STORM
The Emerald Sea

Mark Robinson

First published in 2021

All characters and events in this publication, other than those
clearly in the public domain, are fictitious and any resemblance
to real persons, living or dead, is purely coincidental.

No part of this publication may be reproduced, stored in a
retrieval system, or transmitted, in any form or by any means,
without the prior permission in writing of the author, nor be
otherwise circulated in any form of binding or cover other than
that in which it is published.

For Toby, Archie and Claire

ACKNOWLEDGMENTS

Special thanks must go to my younger son Toby. Your enthusiasm and constant requests to 'write the next chapter Dad!' were all the motivation I needed. Okay, okay, stop asking, I'll try to get the next chapter of "Storm 2" to you before bedtime.

Thanks also of course to Archie for your invaluable help, pointing out all my mistakes and coming up with plot ideas. Your imagination is limitless!

And finally a huge thank you to Claire, not only for your endless support and editorial feedback, but also for designing this book cover. Shiver me timbers, it's m*aaar*velous!

1

The roar of his crewmates filled his ears. Caleb glanced briefly at the man balanced precariously beside him on the side of the ship. He was clinging tightly to the rigging which rose up to the crow's nest high above them. Caleb could see the fear and excitement in his eyes as he placed the knife between his teeth and reached with his free hand for the rope dangling above him. The whole boat shook as another volley of cannon fire shot from the portholes beneath them. Seconds later, splintered holes were punched into the side of their quarry. Caleb noticed their rudder explode, while another cannonball took out the stern mast. There was no hope for them now. The only question was whether they'd surrender immediately or put up a futile resistance.

The sun was beginning to set behind them, flickering a golden orange across the ocean that was deepening in colour with every passing minute. Caleb scanned the opposing ship, feeling some sympathy

3

for the sailors squinting in their direction. They must look a formidable sight, bearing down on the doomed vessel on what must appear to be a sea of fire. Caleb had served on The Cutlass for two years and knew few ships looked more intimidating. She was one of the largest in the Caribbean, towering over most of her victims. The hull had been painted black with tar but at this time of day with the sun dropping towards the horizon it would reflect flashes of deep red, striking fear into their enemies. Even the Jolly Roger, their huge flag adorned with a gruesome skull and crossbones, had been sewn with a black and scarlet cloth that shimmered almost magically and would signify death to anyone unfortunate enough to see it coming their way.

'No pistols,' shouted Jasper on his other side. 'Look, they've only got swords. This'll be over quickly.'

'The captain will have one hidden somewhere,' Caleb warned his friend. Jasper was the only member of the crew younger than himself and he felt he needed to calm his excitement. 'Although he should stick to his sword. He'd be lucky to hit the boat with a gun in this sea.' He looked at the dark clouds approaching. It was going to be an awful night. They crashed down into another trough between the waves before being lifted again by the next. Six more, he thought. Six more waves and they'd be on top of them. He snaked an arm around his own rope and banged the hilt of his sword on the side of the boat. It was a simple blade, old and worn, but it made a heavy thump as he pounded it on the wooden rail. The captain liked them to make a lot of noise when

STORM – THE EMERALD SEA

they took another ship. Scare them witless he'd tell them and the battle was won. Caleb could see the fear in their eyes already and knew Captain Marmaduke was right.

'Ready boys and girls?' shouted Barrowclough behind them, laughing as he said it. The wind had picked up and he had to raise his voice as heavy droplets of rain started to hit their faces. 'Time to make men of you at last. You never forget your first time. Do yourselves proud now. Give no quarter. You put them down and you don't stop fighting until the captain gives the order, hear me?'

Caleb squeezed his hand around his rope. His heart was pounding. He'd seen this dozens of times before. Witnessed the rest of the crew swinging across to attack the enemy, seen firsthand the frenzied fighting as men tried desperately to defend themselves. He'd tended the injured and dying who'd been brought back. But he and Jasper had never been in the boarding party themselves. They'd never come face to face with an enemy and clashed swords knowing it was a fight to the death. Captain Marmaduke had drilled them endlessly, making them swing from their mast to the empty husks of old victims, driving them up and down the rigging a hundred times until they flew like eagles, pairing them off against each other for hours every day practising their swordsmanship. 'Winning battles ain't luck boys,' he'd shout as he sent them up the ropes again. 'The strongest survive. The losers feed the fish.'

Caleb glanced down at the boiling water sandwiched between the two ships. They were nearly on top of them now. Two more waves.

'I said do you hear me?' cried Barrowclough as they rose to meet the next crest.

'Aye, sir!' shouted the two teenagers, and they banged their swords on the ship's rail as they levelled out and plummeted into the trough.

'For the Duke!' screamed Barrowclough even louder over the boom of the hull crashing into the bottom of the wave as they tilted abruptly upwards again.

'The Duke!' yelled the crew. They crested the final wave and Caleb found himself looking down on the other boat from only a few metres away. The first of his pirate crewmates were already leaping. A sudden desire to prove himself swept over him and without pausing to think what he was doing he tightened his grip on the rope and jumped.

It swung him across perfectly, their ship still slightly above their victim, allowing him to drop firmly onto the other's deck. At the back of his mind he was pleased to have landed on his feet and hoped the captain had seen it. The experienced pirate on his left dropped cat-like to the floor but Jasper slipped on the wet planks and collided heavily with some crates. An enemy crewmate saw him stumble and lunged forwards with his sword to strike Jasper while he was down but Caleb reacted more quickly and leaned across to parry the thrust. Momentum was with him and a frenzied excitement overtook him as he slashed and blocked his opponent. His lessons were forgotten as he pushed his assailant back through sheer power alone. The endless hours of drills had ingrained themselves and Caleb was able to react instinctively to each move the enemy made.

Out of the corner of his eye Caleb saw Jasper get up and engage another sailor but he was barely aware of anyone else on the ship as he focussed on the man opposite. His face was mostly covered in a thick olive green bandana, though Caleb could tell he was young. Perhaps even as young as him. Nevertheless, he was good. They'd only been duelling for twenty seconds but it felt like hours and Caleb already knew they were evenly matched. Time and again he checked his opponent's moves, counter attacking with his own thrusts which were similarly met. He wasn't conscious of his stance but a casual observer would have looked on admiringly at the way he'd positioned his body, side on to his challenger to protect his vital organs, weight evenly distributed on both legs which were perfectly bent to keep his balance in the churning sea. The Duke had trained them relentlessly over the last two years and although only fourteen Caleb was now the best swordsman on the crew. Only the captain could better him in a fight, which he frequently did much to the amusement of the rest of the men.

But that was all just training and the Duke had warned him it was no substitute for the real thing. The battle raged on around him, sailors screaming with fury as they fought, the rain falling more heavily. Caleb was oblivious to it all as both swords flew from side to side, their movement a blur in the darkening sky. He wanted to take a closer look at the man facing him but couldn't risk taking his eyes from the two blades. He was aware they were equal in weight and length, both shorter and lighter than many of the swords favoured by the pirate crew. The Duke had watched Caleb's speed and insisted the longer epee weapon would hamper him in a close quarters skirmish. Right now, in the heat of battle, his arm had never been swifter, but the opposing sword flashing at him complemented his every manoeuvre. He was fast realising this fight would come down to stamina alone. Which of them would have the strength to wear the other down. With their lives depending on it Caleb knew neither man would give up easily.

He suddenly sensed a shift in the activity going on around him. The sound of fighting elsewhere on the ship had ceased. He briefly caught sight of Jasper standing nearby watching them, his own blade raised in both hands as he tracked the pair across the deck. His adversary had noticed the same thing and both swordsmen took a step back from each other as they sized up the situation. With relief, Caleb realised the battle had ended. The other ship was beaten and his own crewmates had now circled them and were enjoying the sport. Caleb grinned. It was twenty against one, his opponent was beaten. He pointed the tip of his sword at the man and gave him a small, apologetic shrug. It was over.

The man made the same gesture and showed a wry smile. He let the hilt of his sword roll around his thumb theatrically so it was pointing towards the floor, then tossed it casually to his left hand. Caleb stepped closer to take it but as he did so the man spun it back up and flicked Caleb's own sword away, lunging forward with a right hook that crunched into Caleb's jaw and sent him flying to the ground. His sword spilled onto the deck and skittered away.

Before anyone could react the man had leapt over and thrust his blade at Caleb's neck, stopping the sharp point a hair's breadth from his throat.

No one moved. Caleb's eyes went wide as he looked up at the long blade, wavering very slightly as it hovered above his Adam's apple. His first battle and they'd won the ship but he was going to lose his life. He'd been such a fool. He gulped as he stared at the length of steel, then raised his eyes to meet his enemy's. If he was going to die in front of his crewmates he wasn't going to let them see any fear. Then the man winked at him, withdrew the blade and held out his hand.

Caleb lay on the deck, shamed by his defeat, but took the arm and allowed the sailor to pull him to his feet. He rubbed his jaw and looked away, not wanting to look at the person who'd not only beaten him but had done it in front of the entire crew. A slow clapping sound distracted him and he half turned to see Captain Marmaduke walking towards them, a glint in his eye.

'Met your match at last have we, Master Storm?' He stopped clapping as he stood before them, his craggy face with the white scar on one cheek creased in amusement. 'Your sword,' he said calmly. The man hesitated briefly then offered the hilt to the captain. 'A fine blade,' he said, inspecting it in the dying light. Something caught his eye and he raised an eyebrow. 'Curious,' he said quietly. He looked down at the unarmed man then lifted the curved sword, pressing the point gently into the soft skin beside the shorter man's eye. He slowly twisted the blade round, watching the young man for any sign of fear, but the

9

captive held his nerve and returned Marmaduke's gaze. Unhurriedly the captain slid the sword and hooked it under the sailor's bandana, flicking it off in one deft movement. Caleb gasped. Long wavy red hair which had been piled on the top of his opponent's head fell in cascades to their shoulders. But it wasn't the realisation that he'd been fighting a girl that had shocked Caleb. It was the unexpected recognition that hit him as her face was revealed.

She kept her eyes fixed on Marmaduke long enough for Caleb to catch his breath, then shifted her head a fraction to look past him and directly at Caleb.

'Hello brother.'

2

The penny dropped as Caleb forced his gaze away from Eloise to the captain. 'You knew?'

Marmaduke lifted the girl's sword again and ran his finger along the edge. 'Not until I saw this,' he said distantly. The sharp point of the curved blade glinted viciously in the dying sun. 'We've met before, haven't we you beauty.' Marmaduke absent-mindedly stroked the lightening white scar running down his cheek and Caleb suddenly understood he was talking to the sword and not his sister.

'Father's,' he gasped.

'How is the old scoundrel?' asked Marmaduke, still transfixed by the weapon in his hand.

'Dead,' Eloise replied belligerently. Caleb stared at his twin sister. Could that be true? He hadn't seen his family since he'd been taken two years ago. For the first month he'd longed to return to them. For the second month he'd started to wonder when he'd see them again. By the third the when had become an if.

11

At some point after that, he realised shamefully, he must have forgotten about them and had simply become a part of Marmaduke's crew.

And now. Now he was a pirate. There was no going back. But that wasn't the case for Eloise. Was it? He became conscious of the fact he knew nothing about her. The last time they'd seen each other had been that fateful day. The twelve year old Caleb had been showing off his pick pocketing skills to the other children in St Croix when he'd seen an easy target. The man in the expensive long burgundy coat had been standing with his back to Caleb on the side of the dock watching an argument between a fisherman and one of his customers. Distracted by the quarrel he was ripe for the picking but the second Caleb's hand had reached into the man's pocket he'd felt a vice-like grip on his wrist. He'd looked up into those black eyes and known real fear for the first time in his life.

No matter how much he'd squirmed he couldn't escape that hold. Then, with a terrifying scraping sound that still haunted Caleb to this day, the man had pulled his cruel looking sword from its scabbard. Eloise had run over and kicked the man but he'd brutally slapped her away then laughed in Caleb's face.

'What's it to be, boy?' he'd asked, leering at him. 'Your hand? Or five years hard labour?'

'Wh-what?' Caleb had stuttered, not understanding what he was being asked.

'You heard me boy. You pay for your crimes. Say goodbye to your hand, or work on my ship.' The man had pointed with his sword at the largest boat in the bay. 'Your choice.'

'Y-your ship?' Caleb stammered, reading the name of The Cutlass on its stern.

'Hamish Marmaduke Ó Riain at your service,' the man had replied, giving Caleb a small, mocking bow. 'Captain Marmaduke to you. Now choose.'

He'd lifted the sword and rested the sharp edge on Caleb's forearm. Even then, the young Caleb had been determined not to cry in front of the man. He was scared, petrified even, but he wouldn't show it. Five years. The time was incomprehensible to him. It felt like a lifetime. But he looked at his hand and flexed his fingers, and knew he couldn't bring himself to choose that option.

'The boat,' he'd mumbled quietly. The man had smirked and sheathed his sword, then without a word had dragged Caleb towards a small boat tied to the dock. Three rough looking sailors were loitering next to it chuckling to themselves at the events of the afternoon.

'Stop right there,' had come a shout from behind them. The man had paused, then without letting go of Caleb turned to face the wharf. A tall, red haired man stepped out from the crowd that had been watching. 'Let my son go. I'll pay you for whatever he took.'

Marmaduke gave the man an evil smile. 'The boy's made his choice. He belongs to me now. How much is he worth to you?'

Caleb's father looked from Marmaduke to him and back. 'Name your price,' he said heavily.

'A thousand doubloons,' answered Marmaduke without hesitating. The crowd gasped. Caleb's mouth dropped open. Just one of the Spanish gold coins was a huge sum. He knew then the captain was toying with his father and had no plans to let him go.

Caleb's father knew it too. Drawing his own sword, the beautiful short blade with the ornate carved hilt that Caleb had polished every night, he took another step closer to Marmaduke. 'I guess we'll settle this the old fashioned way.'

Marmaduke threw Caleb behind him to the sailors waiting on the dock and drew his own sword in the same swift movement. 'That's a fine blade you have there,' Marmaduke said admiringly. 'Looks like I'll be taking home two prizes today.'

Caleb's father had pounced like lightening and against anyone else Caleb knew the fight would have been over already, but Marmaduke reacted just as quickly. The two blades flashed as the men sparred, the steel a whirl while they paced back and forth along the wharf. And then it happened. Marmaduke was a fraction slow and Caleb saw his father's sword slash the captain's leg, then in a split second it whipped up slicing right across Marmaduke's face. He jumped, stung by the move, and slowly lifted his hand to his cheek.

The sailor holding Caleb tightened his arm around his neck as he took a small step forward, bracing himself to rush to his captain's aid. But Marmaduke waved at him to stay back. He pulled his hand away, covered in blood. Nodding respectfully to Caleb's father he lifted his sword again. This time Marmaduke attacked furiously, beating Caleb's father back towards the market stalls lining the harbourside. But again momentum turned as the onslaught was checked. Marmaduke was pressed once more. Sweat glistened on both men's foreheads as they clashed. No one dared intervene. Then out of nowhere a cat shot across the cobblestones, a dog tearing after it. The cat ran straight between the two swordsmen but the dog crashed into Caleb's father's legs causing him to stumble slightly. It was only a tiny slip but it was enough. Marmaduke struck, knocking the sword from his father's hand which went sliding away across the ground and disappeared beneath one of the stalls.

'No!' shouted Caleb as Marmaduke advanced on the defenceless opponent.

The captain was breathing heavily. 'End of the road, my friend,' he announced, spitting blood on the stone floor. He lifted his sword to deliver the final killing blow.

'Ten years!' shouted Caleb from the jetty. Marmaduke checked his swing and twisted to inspect the boy. 'Ten years,' repeated Caleb. 'I'll serve on your ship. Just let my father go.'

Marmaduke spat another glob of blood to one side. 'You hear that? He's a brave lad, I'll give him that. He's earned you your life but your boy's mine now. Mine!' he shouted. And he turned and limped back to the boat.

3

All of that seemed a lifetime ago. Caleb's thoughts were overrun with questions about what had happened to Eloise and their father in the last two years.

'But,' he stammered. 'What? H-How? How did you get here?'

'That's obvious isn't it boy?' the Duke reflected. 'She came looking for you.' He turned and threw Eloise's sword to Barrowclough who'd been standing nearby and caught it deftly by the hilt. 'Bring the survivors across. I'll inspect them in the morning. And make sure that one's securely tied,' he added, nodding towards Eloise. 'The rest of you strip the ship. She's taking on water lads so work quickly if you don't want to end up on the bottom of the ocean. I want us away from here within the hour. Caleb, up you go.' He pointed to the top of the mainmast rising high above them, the largest of the three masts on the ship and the only one still in one piece. 'Rigging, sails, anything of value, you know the drill.' He swept his gaze around the deck. 'What are you all standing there for?' he growled. 'Move!'

He strode off towards the captain's quarters while the rest of the crew sprang into action. Caleb hadn't yet recovered from the shock of seeing Eloise again and remained frozen in place. Barrowclough grabbed her arm and shoved her roughly towards The Cutlass which was tied alongside. 'Get to work lad,' he told Caleb. 'Don't want to upset the boss now, do you.'

In half the time they'd been given the conquered ship had been stripped and the crew were all back on board The Cutlass. The threatening storm had passed and a clear night had fallen, the last of the rainclouds now way off in the distance. A myriad of stars lit the sky and the bright moon gave them plenty of light to see by. Barrowclough released the doomed ship and Caleb watched as they slowly drifted apart. The now empty vessel was listing heavily to starboard and the crew started taking bets on how long it would take to go under. Caleb took his chance while they were distracted to slip away from the crowd and seek out the prisoners, all tied back to back in pairs on the forecastle at the front of the ship.

'I'll watch them for a bit,' he told the guard leaning against the foremast. 'Go and place your bet on the scuttling.' The man had taken one look at Caleb then glanced at Eloise.

'Cap'n said you'd be over,' he grinned. 'So long as she stays tied up you can have your little family reunion. But if you want my advice I wouldn't get too attached. The Duke hasn't decided what to do with this sorry lot yet.' He raised his voice so the beaten crew could all hear him. 'Reckon they're all shark bait meself.' He pushed himself up and sauntered over to the others, calling out to ask the odds on the sinking as he went.

'I'll speak to the captain,' Caleb said, crouching down close to his sister. 'Make sure he doesn't throw you overboard.'

'He listens to you does he?' Eloise asked derogatorily. 'What are you going to do? Offer him another five years?'

The comment stung Caleb. He'd done what he'd had to. It had been the only thing he could think of at the time to save their father from the Duke's sword. 'You're not worth five,' he answered. 'Six months max. In fact, he'll probably get so sick of you he'll let me off a year early just to get rid of you.'

Eloise glared at him but then saw Caleb was grinning and she couldn't help softening. 'Not how I planned it. It's good to see you.'

'You planned this?' Caleb asked laughing. 'I'd hate to see what happens when you make it up as you go along.'

'They told me they were a fearsome ship,' she replied sullenly. 'The scourge of the Caribbean apparently. Some scourge they turned out to be.'

'We are fearsome,' complained the sailor with his back to Eloise. Caleb raised an eyebrow at the old man who'd lifted his head and was staring wide-eyed at him. 'Were, anyway,' he added forlornly, before dropping his head again.

They were interrupted by a big cheer. Caleb craned his neck to watch the final death throes of Eloise's boat before it sank beneath the waves. The crew standing on the lower main deck in the middle of the ship all paid and collected on the bets, mostly tobacco or small coins, then slowly settled down to sing some sea shanties. The captain ran a tight ship but they'd fought well this evening and he made sure they were always rewarded after a battle. Caleb knew it was unlikely he'd be disturbed until morning.

'Tell you what lad,' said one of the other captured crewmembers. 'You untie us and we'll take the ship, make you captain. How does that sound?'

Caleb snorted. If they waited for the crew of The Cutlass to fall asleep then maybe they'd kill off a couple of them before the Duke's men fought back, but once they were awake they'd be ruthless. Every prisoner would be painfully dispatched, Caleb among them. He liked the idea of being made captain but only a fool would have taken the sailor up on that offer.

'Next man who suggests something like that, I'll throw them overboard myself,' Caleb replied. The sailor who'd spoken didn't seem too surprised by the answer and after a few quiet grumbles the prisoners settled down for an uncomfortable night. Caleb beckoned Eloise and her partner to shuffle away from the others so they could talk in peace.

'What'll happen to us?' asked the old sailor tied to Eloise once they'd moved. He tried to find a more comfortable position but winced and started coughing uncontrollably.

Caleb shrugged. 'It varies,' he replied once the man had gone quiet. 'Sometimes the captain takes one look at a crew and throws the lot overboard. If you're lucky he'll keep half, offering you the chance to join him.'

'And how does he decide on the half to keep?'

Caleb hesitated. 'He'll pair you off against each other. Sorry,' he added. 'It's cruel but there's too many of you to feed. Plus some of the men like the sport.'

The old man nodded, then started coughing again. 'No one lives forever,' he gasped finally. 'Listen, in case I don't make it –'

'Don't,' Caleb interrupted. 'You can't think like that. It's fifty fifty. Don't give up yet.'

'I'm hurt lad, can't you see?' He leaned to the side, displaying a shirt matted with dried blood. 'Even if I wasn't, I'm an old seadog. He'll want the younger, stronger men. And I'm not a fighter. I'm the cook.'

'Could always use a good cook,' Caleb suggested. 'I'll let the captain know. What's your name.'

'Aye, you're a good lad,' the sailor replied, eyeing Caleb appreciatively. 'Miss Storm said you were worth fighting for.' Caleb looked at his sister who flushed slightly. 'My name's Wade. Torlan Wade, but just Wade will do. Now, listen, we might not have much time. I've kept this secret long enough, I'm not taking it to my grave.'

'Secret?' asked Caleb.

'I wasn't always an old man, you know,' confided Wade. 'I was young too once. Long time ago. I sailed on –.' He paused to look around, then lowered his voice so Caleb had to lean in closer just to hear him. 'A long time ago, way before you two were born, I sailed on The Black Phantom.'

'The Phantom?' laughed Caleb, sitting against the railings lining the deck. A couple of the other prisoners glanced over at the noise then went back to their thoughts. 'That old myth?' asked Caleb. 'There's no such thing, it's just a children's story.'

'Keep your voice down,' urged the old man. 'She was real alright. And she was a beauty. Makes this tub look like a kid's toy.'

'Are you saying Marissa Cortez was a real person?' whispered Caleb.

'Aye,' nodded the old man. 'The legend is true. Cortez was real. The Phantom was real. And so is the Emerald Sea.'

4

'The what?' Eloise asked.

'The Emerald Sea,' Caleb repeated thoughtfully. 'It's not water,' he explained to his sister. 'I've heard the tales. A haul of emeralds so vast it stretches as far as you can see. Like looking out on a sea of green.'

Wade chuckled, then collapsed in a coughing fit again. 'Now that is a kid's story,' he managed after a few minutes. 'There aren't that many gems. But it's still a fair old haul. Emeralds, sapphires, topaz. All greens and blues, glittering like a perfect sea in the evening sun,' he said wistfully. He went quiet. For a moment Caleb thought he'd died but then he lifted his head and showed a renewed fire in his eyes. 'A dozen chests and more. It was a sight to behold, I can tell you.'

'So where is this treasure?' Eloise asked, twisting her neck to get a glimpse of the man she was tied to.

The man gazed up at the clear night sky. 'How's your navigation skills?'

The twins exchanged a look and grinned. 'We can find the buckle on Orion's belt in a thunderstorm,' Eloise replied.

'While wearing blindfolds,' Caleb added. Their father had taught them the stars. Drummed it into them in their lessons, saying the surest way to survive in this life is to know exactly where you're going, and where you've been. Caleb had a brief pang of guilt as he realised he'd not paid attention to the sky for a long time. He sat back and looked up at it now as if seeing it for the first time. The constellations sprang into life, everything still there as he remembered them. The North Star drew his eye first, the Plough pointing straight at it with Cassiopeia further on. Gradually as his eyes became accustomed more and more patterns leapt into view.

'Beautiful aren't they,' said Wade, reading Caleb's thoughts. 'Cortez taught me the wonder of them. Now she was fearsome. Would have seen to your Captain Duke or whatever they call him.' He sighed. 'Ah, but she appreciated beauty too.'

'The gems,' Caleb said.

'The gems,' echoed Wade. 'You know, after she'd hidden them, she sank her ship with all onboard so no one could ever double cross her. I alone was allowed to live.'

'Why you?' asked Eloise.

The old man shrugged, then wheezed painfully as he pressed a hand to his side. 'I've asked myself that every day since. Captain Marissa, she was ruthless, but she kept me alive, taught me the ways of the sea, the winds, the heavens. I was just a boy, younger even than you. But she put her trust in me and told me that one day, when I'm an old man, I could pass on the knowledge of where the stars led.'

'The stars lead to the gems?' asked Caleb, inching forward.

'Aye, the stars. And the map in my –.' He broke off as he began coughing again.

'Shut him up,' grumbled one of the other captives tied up on the deck.

Caleb looked at the old man, concerned by the grey pallor of his skin and by the growing patch of red on his shirt.

'We need to get you looked at,' he said as the coughing subsided.

The man shook his head. 'My – my boot,' he gasped hoarsely, pointing at his right leg.

'Your boot?' Caleb asked looking at the man's feet in the dim light. He hadn't noticed before. Many of the sailors only had the cheapest of deck shoes, or even went barefoot once their soft moccasins had fallen apart. But not Wade, who had on a fine pair of old Scottish brogans. He'd come across Scots and Irish sailors before who'd needed the sturdy leather shoes in their wet, boggy homelands. Caleb wondered if that was where Wade was from or if he'd taken them from another sailor at some point in his life.

'Y-You need to –,' tried Wade, but his strength was failing and he couldn't finish the sentence.

'Wade?' asked Caleb urgently. 'Hang in there. Water, I'll get you some water. Wait here.'

As he jumped up he felt slightly foolish for telling Wade to wait there. The man was badly injured and tied to his sister on a ship full of pirates. He wasn't likely to be running off anywhere any time soon. Caleb skidded down the dozen steps to the main deck where an immense barrel of drinking water was kept. The men usually scooped it up with their hands and Caleb hunted frantically around for a cup. He knew he couldn't leave the prisoners unguarded for long but he couldn't return empty handed either.

He scoured the area looking for anything which would suffice, treading carefully so as not to disturb the members of his own crew who had fallen asleep right there on the open deck. He wondered briefly who was on duty in the crow's nest tonight, the small lookout platform at the top of the mainmast. Hopefully someone who wouldn't care too much about him abandoning his post.

Just then he saw it. A silver cup among the booty they'd salvaged from the sinking ship. The captain knew none of his men would dare touch the haul during the night so it was safe to leave it all out until he could inspect it in daylight. Caleb leapt over Barrowclough's snoring body and scooped it up. He froze as a gold chain slid noisily down the pile. No one stirred but Caleb approached the barrel more cautiously, every creak of the wooden boards making him squirm.

Dunking it quickly in the water, he made his way carefully back up the steps to the foredeck. The prisoners were all where he'd left them, dozing uncomfortably in their pairs. Caleb hurried to his sister and knelt beside Wade, one hand on his shoulder and the other holding the cup to his lips.

'Drink Wade, drink,' he urged. But the old sailor's head was drooped over, his chin resting on his chest.

'Is he – ?' Caleb whispered to his sister.

'Dead,' she confirmed. 'There was nothing I could do.'

Caleb sat on the floor, defeated. It wasn't just that he'd started to like the old man. He'd wanted to hear more tales of his adventures with the famous Captain Cortez and her ship The Black Phantom. But Wade's death meant that his secret, the location of the legendary Emerald Sea, had died with him.

'Get the map,' said Eloise. 'The one he said was in his boot.'

Caleb looked at her, startled. In his rush to get the water he'd forgotten about what Wade had been telling them. He looked round but no one was watching so he crawled forwards and knelt by Wade's foot. Undoing the two buckles on the side, Caleb slipped off the boot and laid Wade's bare foot gently on the deck.

'Found it?' Eloise asked quietly.

Caleb shook the boot upside down hoping the map would fall out but nothing happened. He peered inside but there was nothing there.

'Try the other one,' whispered Eloise.

Caleb nodded and put the boot down, leaning round to his left leg to remove the other one. Again, he laid him down softly. Even though Wade was dead it felt wrong to just carelessly drop his leg and Caleb felt honour-bound to show the old sailor some respect.

'Nothing,' he said, deflated, after searching the second boot. He threw it down next to the first one in disgust. 'He was winding us up the whole time. There is no Emerald Sea, it's all just a myth.'

The two siblings sat there in silence for a minute. Caleb had been convinced by the Wade's story. He'd wanted to believe it so much, he felt a fool for being taken in. He picked up one of the boots again and absentmindedly turned it round in his hands. 'Would have been cool though, wouldn't it,' he said thoughtfully. 'A quest for hidden treasure? Beats attacking other ships for a few scraps of silver. Safer too.'

'You think Cortez was real?' asked Eloise. 'There weren't many women pirates in those days. I like to think she was the fiercest of them all, scaring the life out of all the men she met.'

Caleb smiled ruefully. 'Like you, you mean?'

Eloise scowled. 'Untie me and say that.'

'Maybe I shoul –.' He stopped mid-sentence, staring at the sole of Wade's boot.

'Yes, maybe you should,' Eloise insisted. 'How would you like it, strapped to a dead man all night?'

'Shh,' Caleb told her. 'Be quiet would you. Look at this.' He held up Wade's boot, showing the bottom of it to his sister. 'There's a map of the stars cut into it.'

'So?' asked Eloise. 'Maybe he wasn't so good at remembering them after all.'

'Look more closely,' Caleb insisted.

Eloise gave him a withering look, then glanced down with a resigned sigh. Tiny silver studs had been planted in the leather mapping out a small portion of the night sky. She squinted at the boot, her eyes darting over the image of the stars in the dim light. Caleb smiled as he saw the realisation jump onto Eloisa's face.

'Cassiopeia's the wrong way round,' she said

excitedly. 'The heel. It's on sideways.'

Caleb reached across and twisted the heel so the constellation appeared in its correct position. The boot emitted a barely audible click and a miniature drawer popped out from the side of the heel.

5

'Show me,' Eloise whispered urgently as Caleb took out a small piece of yellowing fabric from the drawer and unfolded it. 'It's starting to get light, the crew will be up soon.'

Caleb glanced at the eastern horizon. His sister was right. The stars had disappeared as the misty light of pre-dawn slowly chased away the darkness. Sunrise couldn't be more than ten minutes away. Hurrying, he turned himself round so he was sitting beside her and flattened out the material on his knees.

'Wade wasn't lying,' Caleb said quietly. 'It's a map.' The rough drawing showed a Y-shaped island, covered in markings and symbols. Most striking was an upside-down heart which filled the gap between the two prongs of the Y. 'There's no name,' observed Caleb. 'Nothing at all on here to say where it is.'

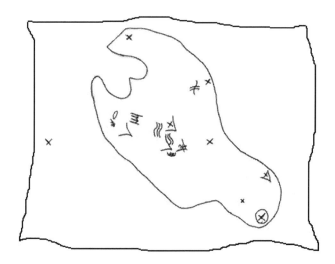

'What's all this other stuff?' wondered Eloise as she studied the markings. 'Does any of it mean anything to you?'

'No,' admitted Caleb. One of the captives sat across from him on the upper deck suddenly jerked his head up from the uncomfortable position he'd been sleeping in, then slowly let it fail again as he dozed back to sleep. His movement disturbed the man tied to him who grumbled quietly before settling. 'It'll have to wait,' Caleb told her, folding the map and stuffing it in his pocket. 'They're starting to wake. Look, I don't know what the Duke has planned but I won't let anything happen to you, I promise.'

Eloise held his gaze for a few seconds, then nodded. There was nothing to say. Whatever happened today would be out of her brother's control. Caleb hesitated, then leaned across and gave Eloise a hug. As he stood and walked back to the foremast to resume his guard duties he couldn't stop thinking about the map in his pocket and had to fight the urge to take it out for another look. He yawned and folded his arms, resting his head against the mast. He hadn't slept since the previous night but was fully alert as thoughts of both the treasure and the danger his sister was in fought for attention in his mind.

Slowly, the crew roused themselves and started moving groggily around the ship. It was shaping up to be a perfect day, the clouds long-since blown away leaving an unblemished blue sky overhead. A gentle breeze filled the many sails of The Cutlass and carried them swiftly southwards. Caleb was convinced everyone who looked in his direction could see the map. It felt like it was burning a hole in his pocket. He forced himself to act as naturally as possible, nonchalantly strolling about the upper deck until he saw Jasper appear a short while after sunrise.

Calling over one of the other crewmates to keep watch on the prisoners, Caleb slid down the steps to the main deck and joined his friend by the water barrel. Jasper scooped up a handful of water to drink, then put both hands in to splash the cold water over his face.

'You boy,' growled a voice behind them. They looked round to see Marmaduke coming out of his cabin. He was pointing at Jasper. 'Get up there and relieve Silas.' He thumbed towards the crow's nest as he strode across the deck, pausing to swear at two of the men who'd been standing chatting. They instantly sprang to work, wary of incurring the wrath of the captain. Caleb knew to look busy or suffer a similar onslaught from the Duke's tongue. He quickly bent to pick up one of the brushes used to scrub the wooden floor and turned away.

'Hold fast, master Storm,' called Marmaduke. Caleb froze then slowly turned to face him. 'Any of that lot cause any trouble in the night?' asked the captain, nodding his head to the captives on the upper deck at the front of the ship.

'No, cap'n,' Caleb replied. 'Quiet as the grave.' Something about the phrase made him shudder as he said it.

Marmaduke grunted then let out a nasty chuckle. 'They won't be so quiet when we send them to the locker, will they lad?'

Caleb looked away in dismay. Davy Jones' locker was the name all sailors gave to the bottom of the sea, where drowned men were said to go. Caleb couldn't bear the thought of Eloise meeting that fate. 'Ah,' said Marmaduke, watching him shrewdly. 'You don't think they should all be punished?'

'Not all of them,' suggested Caleb looking out across the ocean as it glinted in the morning sun. He knew the captain was toying with him but he had no choice but to go along with it. 'We should keep one alive at least. Let them spread the word of how terrifying you are, of how you rule these seas.'

'Got one of them in mind, do you?'

Caleb chose not to answer. The Duke knew what he wanted but anything he said now would be mocked in front of the rest of the crew. Instead, he forced himself to meet the captain's gaze. He realised there and then he would fight to the death to protect Eloise.

Marmaduke held his stare, reading the

determination on Caleb's face. They were interrupted by the sound of footsteps landing lightly beside them.

'Mister Cragen,' Marmaduke acknowledged, not blinking or moving from his scrutiny of Caleb. 'All quiet out there?'

Caleb knew it was futile to glare at the captain any longer. He'd shown his feelings and there was no sense antagonising him. He looked away, taking in the leering features of Silas Cragen instead. He instantly regretted it. Silas was a snake, the one crewmember he'd never got on with. The man delighted in causing trouble. He'd happily torture prisoners, tormenting them before coldly dispatching them. Caleb suspected he'd sell his own grandmother if it got him into Marmaduke's good books. And that was the problem. Whatever else he was, for all his multitude of faults, the obsequious Silas was fiercely loyal to the captain.

'All quiet out there, captain,' Cragen confirmed. 'Not so quiet down here.' He looked at Caleb with a knowing grin. A cold dread crept over him. What had Silas heard during the night? Surely he couldn't have listened in on anything Wade or Eloise had said? 'Up all night, this one,' Silas continued. 'Plotting with that pretty little sister of his.'

Marmaduke dismissed the comment. 'Catching up on the family gossip, that's all. I'm not completely heartless, am I lads?' he asked, raising his voice for the last bit. Caleb realised several other members of the crew had been loitering nearby, watching the three of them curiously. He still couldn't believe Silas could have heard anything but something was telling him this wasn't good. Maybe it was the loathsome way Silas was watching him. He had to get away from this conversation so he could hide the map somewhere safe.

'Wasn't just them what was talking, captain,' Silas continued. 'Seemed the other prisoner with them had a lot to say.'

'It was nothing,' Caleb said quickly. 'He was dying, wanted water, that's all. It didn't make any difference, he didn't make it.'

Marmaduke shrugged dismissively. 'One less sport for the men then.' Caleb didn't like the sound of that. It didn't bode well for the ones who were left if the captain was planning on giving his crew some entertainment.

'That was all, was it?' Silas asked, smirking. Before Caleb could think of what to say, Silas had grabbed his wrist and held it tight against the mast. 'So what was it you put in your pocket?'

6

Marmaduke looked from Caleb to Silas and back, then took a couple of steps forward and reached into Caleb's pocket and fished out the scrap of fabric. Caleb silently cursed himself. He should have hidden it as soon as he could.

'I was going to show it to you later, captain,' Caleb said. He knew the excuse sounded weak. 'Thought you'd want to see it in private, without the other men knowing.' He glared at Silas as he said it, hoping his obvious distrust of the first mate would sound convincing.

Marmaduke turned the map around in his hands. 'Oh, you did, did you?' He waved the map in the air and raised his voice. 'You hear that boys? Master Storm here doesn't trust you.'

'I trust the men, sir,' Caleb protested, yanking his arm away from Silas's grip and rubbing his wrist in annoyance. 'Just not him.' Silas spat on the floor by Caleb's foot in response. Caleb looked around at the crew nervously. He hoped they'd be on his side. He'd always got on well with everyone and hoped they considered him a popular member of the crew, unlike Silas who no one would miss. But he also knew those loyalties would disappear in an instant if the captain ordered it.

'That old sea dog tell you where this is?' asked Marmaduke, studying the piece of fabric.

'No,' admitted Caleb. 'He died before he could tell us anything.' Since taking him away from his family, Marmaduke had been a fair commander. Hard, sure, and ruthless, but he'd protected Caleb while he was younger and taught him the skills he needed to survive on the pirate ship. Despite everything, Caleb had learned to respect the captain and under any normal circumstances would be completely loyal to him. But Wade had kept the treasure secret for his whole life. He'd entrusted that secret to him and Eloise alone. Caleb couldn't divulge it now, certainly not in front of Silas.

'Barrowclough,' shouted Marmaduke. 'Change of course. Ready the sails, set your heading for the North East.'

'You know it?' Caleb asked incredulously.

Marmaduke ignored him, continuing to inspect the map as Barrowclough began calling out instructions to the crew. Caleb was confused. Did the captain recognise the island? Or was this some ploy to make Caleb think he did. Or were they going somewhere else entirely that had nothing to do with the treasure. He wasn't sure what to believe but feigning ignorance seemed like the safest way to survive this.

'Sorry captain. If I'd known it was important I'd have brought it straight to you. It didn't seem that urgent at the time.'

'You're a terrible liar, Storm. Tie him to the mainmast Silas. Then fetch his sister down here. This lad needs to be taught a lesson.'

Caleb put up a half-hearted resistance as Silas dragged him to the mast. He knew it was futile to fight it. Marmaduke would only call in others to help and it would only worsen whatever punishment was coming his way. He lifted his chin defiantly as Silas roughly pulled his arms around the mast so he was hugging it, then bound them securely. He leaned in close to Caleb's ear as he was doing it. 'This should be fun,' he leered.

'I'll get you for this, Cragen,' Caleb hissed.

'You gotta survive first, boy,' he sniggered, then left to fetch Eloise.

Caleb looked around the deck hoping desperately that someone might come to his aid but the crew were avoiding his eye. Whatever the captain had planned Caleb was going to have to face it alone. His guess was the cat o'nine tails, the nine-stranded whip Marmaduke sometimes used to maintain discipline. He'd never been on the receiving end before but had witnessed it twice. One man had received forty lashes then later died from infections on his lacerated skin but the other had survived, just. Right now, fifty-fifty odds seemed as good as he was going to get.

'Get off me,' protested Eloise as Silas manhandled her down the steps then shoved her in front of the captain. Marmaduke looked her up and down, judging her. He'd discarded her bandana the night before, leaving her fiery red hair cascading over her shoulders. Otherwise she was dressed like any of the lower ranked men on the boat with loose trousers, a baggy white shirt and a brown waistcoat to keep off the chill breeze at night. A slim satchel, her only belongings other than her confiscated sword, had been taken and added to the booty piled up on the deck.

'What?' she asked Marmaduke aggressively as he surveyed her. 'Never seen a pirate before?'

He gave an amused grunt at her confidence. 'You knew the man who gave you this?' he asked, holding up the map.

Eloise gave a quick glance at Caleb then returned her attention to the Duke. She shrugged. 'He was one of the crew.'

'He say where this is?'

'In the sea,' answered Eloise belligerently.

Marmaduke whipped his arm up without any warning and slapped Eloise with the back of his hand. She fell to the ground, blood forming at her lip. 'Don't get smart with me girl,' Marmaduke warned. 'Get up.'

Eloise gritted her teeth and stood before him again, jutting out her chin in the same determined look of defiance Caleb had given. 'I'll ask you again. Did he ever mention this island?'

She shook her head. 'Not to me. He was a quiet one from what I could tell, never said much to anyone.'

Marmaduke nodded. 'And last night? Before he died, what did he say then?'

'Not a lot,' Eloise answered. 'He was hurt. Cal got

him some water but he died before he could get back.'

The captain looked from one to the other and shook his head. 'There's something you're not telling me. And I know how to make you talk. Gentlemen,' he shouted. 'Gather round. There's some bonus entertainment for you all today before the main event. We're going to have us a good old fashioned keelhauling!'

He laughed and walked over to Caleb, who had gone white. 'What's the matter boy? Thought you were going to get off lightly with a few strokes of the whip? Let's see what you have to say after you've been dragged beneath the ship a few times.'

He glanced at Eloise as he undid the knot holding Caleb to the mast. 'Don't want you getting too warm down there my dear. Lose the waistcoat.' Caleb suddenly realised he wasn't going to be alone. Marmaduke planned to torture both of them. Eloise reluctantly undid her belt and dropped it to the floor, then shrugged off her waistcoat. She knew if she didn't someone would cut it off her anyway.

Marmaduke pushed Caleb face to face with Eloise and tied his hands behind her back. Walking round to the other side, he took the rope the sneering Silas was offering and bound Eloise's wrists securely.

'Bet you two haven't been this close since you were in the womb,' said Marmaduke, testing the knots. 'Not so warm and comfortable today I'm afraid. Silas, their feet.'

'I'm sorry,' Caleb whispered as Silas wrapped more rope around their legs, binding them tightly.

'There wasn't anything you could do,' Eloise told

him. 'Ever seen this done before?'

'No,' Caleb admitted. 'Heard about it though. If they drag us quickly, we scrape against the bottom of the ship and get torn to shreds. If they go slower we might not get hurt as bad but there's a chance we'll drown. Either way, not good.'

Eloise nodded.

'I know one thing,' Caleb murmured quietly so no one else could hear. 'Whatever happens, I'm not telling that swag-bellied, pox-breathed scurvy maggot a thing.'

Eloise let out a small snort. 'Pox breathed? I don't remember you being so good at swearing before. You've changed.'

'Two years living with pirates,' Caleb explained. 'I've learned a lot of new words.'

'I bet you have.'

They were interrupted by one of the crew grabbing Caleb by the shoulder and forcing a long rope under his arms and around his chest before pushing them both to the deck. Another man bound their legs with a second rope then strapped a cannonball on for additional weight. 'All set captain,' he announced when he was done.

'Bring them here,' ordered Marmaduke. Three of the sailors tugged on the first rope which had been fed over the yard arm on the mast, hoisting Caleb and Eloise off the ground and into the air. Silas stepped forward and swung them across the rail so they were left dangling above the sea. Caleb leaned his head over Eloise's shoulder to look down at the churning water as the boat, under full sail, swiftly made its way north. The rope tied to their feet disappeared from view. He knew it would have been fed beneath the keel, with more men ready to pull it on the other side of the ship. Fear gripped him and he looked at Eloise to see how she was coping. She locked eyes with him, her teeth gritted.

Marmaduke perched himself casually on the rail next to them. 'Just to let you know,' he said with an evil glint in his eye, 'the hull's not been scraped for years. Those barnacles will be especially sharp by now. Let 'em drop!'

A moment later, Caleb felt his stomach rise into his chest as they plummeted, crashing into the racing water.

7

The weight of the cannonball pulled them down but then Caleb felt the rope tugging under his shoulders and a moment later they broke the surface. The shock was already passing but Caleb was filled with dread at what was to come.

'Take some deep breaths,' gasped Eloise. 'We need as much air as we can get.'

Caleb nodded and took two or three big breaths. He felt the rope around his legs go abruptly taut. 'Now!' he warned, then sucked as much air in as he could. A second later they were both yanked under, their feet pointing at the bottom of the ship as the rope pulled them towards it.

Holding firmly onto Eloise, Caleb forced her round so she was beneath him. She tried to fight it but he squeezed her more tightly until she stopped resisting and let the rope take them. He felt his feet bump into the hull and braced himself for what was to come. The cannonball was dragging him down but the taut rope around his chest ensured he stayed pressed in close to the ship. A thousand needles suddenly stabbed into his calves and a mouthful of bubbles escaped as he cried out in pain.

With his eyes clamped shut he arched his back to try to keep Eloise's bare arms away from the razor-sharp limpets stuck to the bottom of the ship. The move spared them both momentarily but the relief was short-lived. He felt the jagged edges tear through his shirt and pierce his skin, scraping agonisingly up to his shoulder blades. Below him, his feet reached the turn, moving blessedly into clear water, but it was little consolation as the rest of his body, wracked with pain, grated along the bottom edge.

Caleb felt himself pulled around the bottom keel of the ship. They were now being hauled feet first up the other side. His head a whirl of confusion as the sea poured up his nose and bubbles frothed around him. It was excruciating and he couldn't stop himself letting out a small puff of breath, just managing to stop himself before he exhaled fully. He had to hang on long enough to reach the surface or he'd drown.

He couldn't see Eloise but could feel her holding him and her presence gave him strength. They were past halfway and as the sharp edges of the barnacles cut again into his calves he knew he had to survive. He hadn't seen his sister for two long years, he wasn't about to lose her now. His back screamed from the endless stinging but the gloom of the depths was easing as they were dragged relentlessly upwards.

And then it was suddenly over as they broke the surface. Feet first, they were heaved upwards by the sailors until they were left dangling upside down at the level of the men on the deck. The seawater in his nose made Caleb's head feel like it was going to explode and was almost worse than the agony coming from his back. They twisted slowly, swinging gently in the breeze as The Cutlass continued its journey north.

Gradually, the fog cleared and the men onboard came into focus. Caleb could see the pity in their eyes and glanced down to see bright red spots of blood splattering onto the water below.

'Are you okay?' Eloise asked worriedly.

'Fine,' Caleb managed to gasp. 'It's just pain, right?'

'Mister Storm!' Marmaduke said gently. 'Enjoying the tickle of the ship?'

'It's not as painful as listening to Silas,' Caleb called.

Marmaduke chuckled. 'You're a brave lad, I'll give you that. Now tell me, what did he tell you about the island?'

'I swear,' Caleb replied. 'If there was anything else I'd tell you. Have I ever failed you? The old guy knew he was dying so gave us the map. I went to fetch water but when I got back it was too late, he was dead. That's it. There's nothing else I can tell you.'

'Maybe,' Marmaduke said thoughtfully. 'Maybe not.' He sat on the railing looking out to sea, deciding what to do with them.

'If he puts us down again,' whispered Eloise, 'I'll take it.'

'No,' Caleb replied. 'One of us needs to survive. If I make it then get me to Tarian, the ship's carpenter.

He's the best healer on the ship.'

Eloise didn't get a chance to argue. Marmaduke had reached a decision. 'Been a while since we had a good keelhauling,' he told the men standing nearby. 'Shame to stop now. Send them down.'

'No!' shouted Caleb as the rope holding them up was slowly released and their heads dropped towards the water. 'I don't know anything!'

'I believe you,' called Marmaduke. 'The first time was to find out what you know. This one's for punishment. The third and fourth, they'll just be for fun.'

The last thing Caleb saw before his head dunked below the surface was Silas's leering grin, mocking him as the ordeal began again. The sight brought out a renewed anger in Caleb. Whatever happened, he would get revenge on him, whatever it took. They hit the side of the hull side on, Caleb's arm taking the brunt of it. There weren't as many limpets here but in a way that made it worse, with one cutting deeply into his flesh as he tried to push Eloise away to safety.

The rope beneath his armpits pulled them down and once more the serrated shells scraped mercilessly across his back. He winced through gritted teeth as they went. He couldn't be sure, it was all so disorientating being upside down, but it felt slower this time. The pain was the same, the rough hull lacerating his skin on top of the cuts from the first run but something was telling him it still wasn't quite as bad as it could be. The cannonball was dragging them down, away from the ship, so the cuts weren't as deep as before.

But that could only mean one thing. The suffering would last longer. Much longer. Would he be able to hold his breath? Would Eloise? He relaxed his grip on her slightly, conscious of squeezing the air out of her if he held on too tightly. This would be a different type of torment, a slow, cruel voyage into the depths. Everything was getting darker but Caleb couldn't tell if that was because they'd nearly reached the bottom or if it was because he was starting to black out.

Without warning his head smacked into the bottom beam running the length of the ship. The impact almost knocked him out cold and he saw stars of light dancing around him. He followed them deliriously, his thoughts taking him away from the present predicament as their conversation with Wade unexpectedly came back to him. The stars. Whatever else the map showed, he was sure Wade was trying to tell them something about the importance of the stars. Other images flashed through his mind. Their father teaching them the constellations. Barrowclough showing him how to navigate. He was vaguely aware they were now travelling up the other side of the hull and that the pain had stopped. His body had gone limp but deep down some instinct was telling him to hang on, to keep holding onto his last breath.

With complete surprise they splashed back into the open air. Groggily, his head pounding, he lifted his eyes to look at Eloise. Her bedraggled hair was hanging around her shoulders, which he suddenly noticed were red with blood.

'You turned us round,' he accused, panting with the effort.

'You're not getting all the glory,' she gasped. 'I didn't think you'd make it. Had to protect you.' Her head collapsed onto his shoulder with the effort from talking, both breathing heavily as they were hoisted level with the deck.

'You made it,' Caleb heard someone say. It was probably Marmaduke but he didn't have the energy to look. He rested his head against Eloise's and waited, limply, to be sent down for a third time.

'Again?' came Silas's eager voice.

'No. Bring 'em on board,' ordered Marmaduke. Caleb was barely aware of them being swung across the railings, then the rope was lowered and they were dumped unceremoniously onto the floor. Exhaustion overwhelmed him and he was struck by a coughing fit, spitting out water as he struggled for breath. Eloise was still trapped beside him, brother and sister uncomfortably trussed together, blood dripping from both their backs onto the wet wooden planks.

He was aware of a shadow passing over them, blocking out the glare of the dazzling sun to the east. Looking up, he saw Marmaduke crouched down, the map in one hand, a long knife in the other. He twisted the blade casually, then used the sharp tip to point at the upside-down heart on the fragment of fabric.

'Pretty unusual marking, don't you think?' Marmaduke asked quietly. 'Ever seen anything like it?'

Caleb shook his head.

'I have,' Marmaduke told them. 'Claw Island. Ain't nowhere else like it. As you're approaching the bay, the reef opens out in front of you like a cold, blue

47

heart. She's beautiful, but treacherous.' He tilted the knife down and used it lift Eloise's chin. 'Much like you I'd wager.'

'You know it?' asked Caleb. 'Then why did you –?'

'I wanted to see what you knew.' He shrugged. 'Seems you didn't know anything after all. You need to learn your history, boy. Could have saved you a lot of pain. This symbol here,' he added, leaning in close so no one but Caleb and Eloise could hear. 'That's the mark of Cortez.'

'Cor – Cortez?' spluttered Caleb.

'Aye. Marissa Cortez. Terror of the high seas forty years ago, and last known possessor of the Emerald Sea. Ah, but I can see from the look in your eye you already knew that, didn't you lad?'

8

Caleb closed his eyes and swore quietly to himself. He should have known Marmaduke would be familiar with the legend. If only he'd given him that information sooner, it would have earned the captain's trust again. And spared them the agony of the keelhauling.

He opened his eyes to see the captain's knife right in front of him. Whatever he was planning for them next couldn't be good, whatever it was.

'I – I didn't,' started Caleb.

'Shh, now,' Marmaduke growled. 'Yes you did. But can't say I blame you, I'd have done the same myself.' He paused, then slid the knife down to the ropes binding them together and sawed through them in a few quick thrusts. Caleb rolled onto his back away from Eloise but then howled out in pain as his shredded flesh rubbed against the deck. Carefully, he twisted himself onto his hands and knees, waiting for the surge of heat on his raw skin to subside.

'Get yourselves looked at,' growled Marmaduke at them as he walked off. 'You'll need all your strength when we get to Claw Island.' Silas, who had been standing nearby, spat on the floor next to them then sauntered off after the captain.

'I don't get it,' Caleb said, still swaying on all fours. 'Why's he letting us go?'

Eloise sat up and began pulling the remnants of rope from her wrists and ankles. 'He must think we know something,' she answered warily.

'But what?' asked Caleb. He felt faint, still disorientated from the ordeal and just wanted to go and curl up in a corner. 'We don't know anything.'

'So long as he thinks we do, he'll keep us alive,' Eloise told him. 'Here, let me help you.' She shuffled over and loosened the scraps of rope wrapped around Caleb then helped him to his feet. He nearly collapsed to the floor again as a fresh wave of pain almost caused him to black out.

'Drink this,' came a gruff voice next to them. Eloise looked up uncertainly. A giant of a man was looming above her, his huge knotted beard reaching down to his ample belly. He was holding out a cup in one hand but bent as he spoke to pick up the cannonball. Eloise had untied it from Caleb's feet and it was starting to roll across the deck. Hanging from his massive hand the heavy metal ball looked insignificant and he effortlessly swung it around like a child's toy as he spoke. 'Relax, it's just rum. It'll take the edge off.'

She took a sip, then coughed as the strong alcohol hit the back of her throat.

'Aye, it's a bit rough, but it'll numb the pain.' Eloise felt the warmth run down inside to her stomach and held the cup to Caleb's lips. He took a big gulp, then gagged as it hit him, nearly spitting it out again.

'Careful now, don't waste it,' warned the man.

'Tarian?' asked Eloise.

The man nodded, then took Caleb from her, crouching to let him flop over his shoulder then standing as if Caleb weighed nothing. 'Can you walk?' he asked Eloise.

'I'm fine,' she replied. 'He took the brunt of it.'

'Doesn't look like it from here. You're a brave lass. Come on, this way.' He led her to a step ladder which disappeared down into the ship's hold. It creaked under his weight but held as he lowered himself into the dark space. He had to be careful not to bump Caleb's head on the opening, or scrape his back on any of the rungs as they descended. Eloise felt a little light-headed as she followed, concentrating fully on each step.

Reaching the bottom she turned round to discover they were on the gun deck. Rows of cannons lined the space, eight on each side. Their hatches were closed but a dim light was being cast from a giant cauldron in the centre of the room. Tarian tossed the cannonball he was still carrying into a corner then lowered himself onto the next stepladder leading down to the 'tween deck. When Eloise joined him, she saw half the space filled with hammocks and the front crammed with storage boxes. Grain spilled from a sack and the smell of food which was well past its best invaded her senses.

Tarian wasn't stopping there though. He was already making his way with Caleb down the next ladder. They were deep in the bowels of the ship now. Eloise wasn't surprised to see this was by far the tallest level on the boat. They were often built that way but the extra height came at a cost. Water sloshed around the rear of the cargo space, which was filled with barrels and more boxes. In the middle was the firebox feeding the cauldron two floors above. But when she turned towards the front she was startled by the scene. An extra floor had been built a step above the actual bottom of the ship, ensuring everything this end remained dry. A large worktop filled centre of the space, with an array of tools strapped to the wall on one side.

Opposite, four long shelves stretched as far as she could see in the darkness. They were crammed with items, a lot of which Eloise couldn't identify. At the end, right up in the bow, was an enormous hammock.

'Did you build all this?' she asked in wonder.

'The men don't like coming down here,' Tarian told her. 'Could be the water, or the rats.'

'Or you?' she asked, giving him a knowing smile.

'Aye, that might have something to do with it too,' he grinned. 'The other levels are too low, this suits me better.' He swept the contents of the table to one end then laid Caleb on it, face down. He let out a low groan but otherwise didn't move.

'He's not going anywhere, let's have a look at you first.' Tarian pointed to a stool then went to collect a jar from the top shelf. Eloise sat down gingerly. She ached everywhere but knew she'd still got off relatively lightly compared to what Caleb had endured. A sudden cheer from above deck made her jump and she looked at Tarian questioningly.

'Looks like your shoulders took the brunt of it,' observed Tarian, reappearing behind her with a small lamp. He was careful not to touch her as he inspected her wounds. 'Your shirt's shredded. I'm going to cut it open so I can get a good look at the damage. Is that okay?'

'Do what you have to,' Eloise told him, leaning over and resting her arms and head on the table. She'd only just met him but despite his intimidating size and gruff manner she already sensed he was someone she could trust. Caleb had specifically asked for him, so if he was good enough for her brother then he was good enough for her.

Ever so carefully, so delicately that she hardly even noticed, Tarian sliced down the remnants of her shirt and folded the material to each side, leaving the top of her back exposed. 'These cuts don't look too deep,' he said reassuringly. 'Should heal in a couple of days.' He walked off towards the middle of the room. Eloise turned her head to watch him. In the gloom of the hold it was hard to tell what he was doing. He appeared to be crouched down on the edge of his raised platform stirring the water sloshing around in the bottom of the boat. She quickly looked down again as he stood up and made his way back to her.

'This will sting,' he warned, and before she could reply he tipped the contents of the pail he was carrying over her back. 'Salt water,' he explained. 'Magical the way it can heal. Looks better already. Washed off most of the blood anyway. And now, this will feel a lot better.' He picked up the jar he'd left on the table and unscrewed the lid, dipping in one of his huge fingers. He smeared it thickly over the cuts. Eloise winced at the initial touch but then instantly felt relief as the cool balm took effect.

'That feels wonderful,' murmured Eloise, her head still buried in her arms. 'What is it?'

'Secret recipe. Don't tell the rest of the crew or they'll all want some. Okay, you're done. Don't move for a few minutes, let it soak in. I've another shirt around here somewhere you can put on once it's dry.'

He disappeared further up into the compartment and rummaged for a few minutes among the boxes stored there. 'I know it's here somewhere. Kept it from a cargo we captured a couple of months ago. Ah, here we are. Knew it would come in handy.' He held up a pristine lady's white frilly blouse, patterned with lilac flowers and a pink hem .

Eloise raised an eyebrow as he placed it on the table in front of her. 'Really?'

'It's clean. Not often you can say that about clothing on this tub. We'll find something more macho for you once you're healed. And before you complain,' he added, pointing at Caleb, 'you wait until you see the one I've got for him.'

9

Tarian had warned Caleb it could be a week before he was recovered enough to go outside. Caleb had been determined to prove him wrong and only three days later climbed stiffly up the ladder into the open air. He left the billowy pastel yellow blouse behind that Tarian had insisted he wear while his cuts healed. He'd endured enough in the last few days without being ridiculed by the crew as well.

Jasper saw him emerge from the hold and immediately slid down the steps from the upper deck to join him. 'You're okay!' he exclaimed. 'Sorry mate, I saw the whole thing from the crow's nest. I came to see you as soon as I got down but you were out of it. Tarian told me not to bother you for a bit. How is it?'

'Sore,' admitted Caleb, shielding his eyes from the glare. After spending so long trapped in the gloom below, the outside world was almost too much for him to bear. 'It's more of a dull throbbing now. I'll live.' The intense sun was blinding but he noticed

Silas standing up near the foremast giving him an amused wave. Caleb turned away, ignoring him. Getting revenge on that loathsome creature would have to wait until he'd regained his strength. 'What happened to the other crew?' he asked Jasper instead.

'Oh, the captain was real generous with them,' replied his friend sarcastically. 'He waited until we could see an island. Way off in the distance it was. Then he gave them all a choice. Dance with Jack Ketch or take a swim.'

'Let me guess,' said Caleb. Dancing with Jack Ketch was another way of saying they'd be hanged, a fate that spread fear into the toughest of pirates. 'They all chose to jump?'

'Of course,' shrugged Jasper. 'But then Silas pulled out his knife and gave them all a few cuts before they went in. Can't see that many would have made it before the sharks were drawn to the scent.'

Caleb chanced another look in the direction of the foremast. Silas had gone back to berating poor Alon Jaladri, one of the gunner's assistants, and was now ignoring the two of them. 'Something's got to be done about him,' Caleb said with disgust.

'Yeah, well, don't let the Duke hear you say that, he – '

'Don't let the Duke hear what?' came a voice behind them. They spun round to see Marmaduke coming from the Captain's Quarters at the rear of the ship.

'I – we – ' stuttered Jasper.

'I was just saying I'm feeling stronger, cap'n,' Caleb answered. 'Ready for duty.'

Marmaduke looked him up and down, then nodded appreciatively. 'You're a strong lad, Storm. I like that in my crew. Report to Barrowclough, he'll find some work for you. And as for you, Master Lorcan,' he added, looking at Jasper, 'aren't you supposed to be scrubbing the upper deck?'

'Aye, sir, on my way sir,' Jasper answered quickly, taking his chance to escape.

'Land ahoy!' came a sudden shout from above them before Caleb had a chance to leave. Everyone on deck looked up to see where the man in the crow's nest was pointing. The helmsman appeared next to Marmaduke and handed him a telescope. Without answering, Marmaduke snatched it and walked to the ship's rail, extending the scope and peering through it.

'Looks like you've recovered just in time Mister Storm,' he said, a satisfied grin on his face. 'Why don't you climb up to the nest to relieve Magnus. You'll get a good view of the heart of the island as we approach.'

For a second Caleb wondered what he meant, then was reminded of the map that had been taken from him. This must be Claw Island. He nodded understanding to the captain then stepped over to the main mast and began climbing. It was slow going. Normally Caleb would fly up, able to reach the top quicker than anyone else onboard, but right now, with his wounds strapped tightly by Tarian, every painful step was a struggle.

He gritted his teeth and kept going, not just because the captain had ordered him. His eyes were already getting used to the bright sunlight again and he desperately wanted to see this. Claw Island, home to the treasure of the Emerald Sea. By the time he made it and had sent Magnus back down they'd covered a quarter of the distance, and from his high vantage point he had a perfect view of the approaching island.

From the direction they were coming Caleb could clearly see the two arms of the Y shape jutting out towards him. In between was a sight he could never have imagined. The bay which filled the gap was carved in two by a jagged reef cutting them off from the beach behind it. On the seaward side the water was a deep navy blue but from the sharp line of the reef onwards it changed to a magical turquoise. That wasn't the most striking feature though. The shape of the reef, along with a shorter spit of land that stabbed out from the middle of the beach, made the whole thing look like a heart. An icy, blue heart.

Caleb wished he had a pencil on him so he could make some notes. He'd lost the map but there could be some clues here, an insight into the mystery of where the treasure might be hidden. He'd have to rely on his memory and focussed on taking everything in. The steepness of the slopes. The change in colour and density of the vegetation. The fissures in the cliff face, some of which may just lead into larger caves, hidden from view. Even the way the waves crashed ominously onto the reef, where they broke and disappeared leaving the mesmerising turquoise water beyond.

By the time the ship was pulling into the bay, the two prongs of its Y shape gliding past them, he felt he knew the island as well as he was ever going to.

Barrowclough was skilfully steering them to a gap of calm water which cut through the curling waves crashing on the reef on either side. Caleb glanced down and saw the crew all in position, ready to drop the sails as soon as they were in the sheltered turquoise water beyond. Everyone was clearly excited to be making land after their long stint at sea.

'Clearer water to starboard,' he shouted down to Barrowclough, who acknowledged him and steered away from the rocks Caleb had seen submerged ahead of them. A minute later he gave the command and the men quickly and efficiently lowered the sails, while another two released the anchor, gently bringing the boat to a stop.

'Nicely done Mister Barrowclough,' Marmaduke called from the foredeck at the front of the ship. 'Magnus, Jasper, ready the tender. And you,' he shouted, looking at Caleb high above. 'What are you still doing up there, get down here.'

Caleb didn't need telling twice. Climbing over the railings of the crow's nest would hurt, as would clambering down the rigging, but he didn't want to miss this trip. The pinnace, the small wooden boat they used to ferry men and cargo to and from land, could only carry twelve men and Caleb had to make sure he was one of them.

He needn't have worried. 'Go and fetch your sister,' Marmaduke ordered when he gingerly dropped onto the main deck. 'I want you two with me.'

Caleb hurried to the hatch leading inside the ship and slid down the ladder to each level. The scratches on his legs were a vivid red but for the most part were healing well. Tarian was more concerned with the state of his back but the wounds had been well cleaned and were now tightly bound. So long as Caleb took care not to aggravate them he ought to make a full recovery.

'Eloise,' Caleb called as he landed in the hold. 'We're here. Captain wants us to go ashore with him.'

'You sure you're up to it?' Tarian asked him.

'Don't have a choice,' Caleb answered, collecting his leather bag from one corner. Eloise did the same, putting on the waistcoat she'd managed to retrieve following their ordeal and lifting her own bag over her shoulder before putting her foot on the first rung of the ladder.

'Wait,' Tarian ordered. 'Captain's got your sword, right?' he asked her. Eloise nodded. The curved blade had been taken by Marmaduke the night she'd been brought on board and she hadn't seen it since. Although allowed to move freely around the ship, she was still technically a prisoner and was not allowed a weapon of her own.

'Take this,' Tarian said, holding out a hairbrush. 'Made it for you specially, thought it might come in handy.'

'A brush?' Eloise asked sceptically. 'Er, thanks.'

'Twist the handle and pull,' Tarian told her. She did as he said, amazement on her face as she withdrew a sharp knife. 'Don't use it unless you need to,' advised Tarian. 'Best if you don't draw too much attention to it.'

'It's beautiful,' Eloise replied, fixing the handle back into place to hide the blade.

Tarian shrugged, embarrassed. 'I like to make

stuff,' he said modestly. 'Didn't forget about you either,' he said, reaching his hand out to Caleb.

'A belt?' Caleb asked, looking at the fancy plaited leather strap. 'Thanks but I've got one.'

'Got one that unwinds into a ten metre long cord have you?' Tarian asked him. 'A hollow cord that is, so if you ever need to swim down to the sea bed, you can put one end in your mouth and, so long as the buckle end stays above the water, you'll be able to breathe through it.'

'No way,' Caleb marvelled, holding the belt up and looking at it in wonder. 'How on earth did you make this?'

'Never you mind,' Tarian answered. 'Haven't tested it mind. Don't know how long it'll last before water gets in. Might prove useful in an emergency. There's more too. See the clasp? That can act as a catapult.'

'A cata –,' started Caleb, laughing. 'You're joking.'

'The other end of the belt is a weighted hook, see?' Tarian continued, ignoring Caleb. 'You take that and drop it in the clasp. Then just pull back and aim. I expect it'll take a bit of practice but once you get the hang of it you never know, you may find a use for it. And if all else fails it'll keep your trousers from falling down.'

'Tarian,' grinned Caleb, tying the belt around his waist. 'You're a genius. If we make it out of this alive I'll –'

'Storm!' bellowed Marmaduke from two floor above.

'Better go, wish us luck,' Caleb said, following his sister up the ladder.

Tarian watched him disappear through the hatch in the ceiling. 'Good luck,' he muttered softly. 'You're going to need it.'

10

The small wooden rowing boat caught a wave and surged the last few metres towards shore. The bow buried itself in the sand as it slid to a stop and the men all jumped out to pull it further up the beach. Caleb wasted no time in joining them. He'd been forced to spend the journey from The Cutlass facing the captain. Marmaduke had sat with his hand on the tiller guiding them in while the rest of the crew rowed, with Caleb and Eloise in the final row of seats. The Duke hadn't taken his eyes off Caleb's for the duration.

Once they were safely away from the ebb and flow of the sea Caleb scanned the beach and surrounding tree line. The island appeared to be deserted. The ship anchored safely in the bay was the only other sign of human life. If they didn't have the map he'd have wondered if anyone had ever stepped foot on this shore.

Marmaduke took out Wade's map and held it up,

his eyes flicking between the old piece of fabric and the hills beyond. Smiling to himself, without saying a word he pointed towards one of the peaks. The other men obediently began trudging across the sand in that direction. Caleb and Eloise stayed close together in the middle of the group, with Silas and Marmaduke bringing up the rear. They were soon deep into the undergrowth, the men at the front hacking a way through thick knots of grass. The trees were so densely packed overhead that the sun was almost completely blocked out. An eerie coolness fell on them and some of the men looked at each other nervously in the half light.

Caleb alone felt relieved, smiling to himself as he walked. The beating heat of the sun had been making his bandages itch like crazy and for the first time in days he was starting to forget about the ache from his wounds. They were still tender but he was healing quickly and felt confident that in another day or two he'd be back to full strength.

The men in front suddenly broke through into a clearing. They paused, waiting for instructions on where to head next while Caleb and Eloise, the next few men then finally Silas and the Captain pushed past the last of the scrub into the open.

'Silas, tie them,' Marmaduke ordered while he again consulted the scrap of fabric. Caleb caught a brief glimpse of the map with its strange symbols drawn on before he saw Silas walking towards him, grinning as he unhooked a long coil of rope from his hip. He expertly tied it around Caleb's waist, then walked the three paces to Eloise and wrapped it around her in the same way, fixing a knot front and back to keep her in place.

'What's going on?' Caleb asked, turning to Marmaduke.

'The only reason you're still alive, boy, is because these markings show some kind of danger up ahead. The map's not clear what. Maybe that old man told you what to expect, maybe he didn't. Either way I'm not risking good men on this. You're expendable.'

Caleb frowned but said nothing. Eloise glared at Silas, clearly furious to be trussed up like a chicken about to be thrown in the pot. Marmaduke ignored them both, turning a full three hundred and sixty degrees as he scanned the tree line. Finally satisfied he lifted a finger and pointed towards a gully dropping between the two smallest hills they could see from their current viewpoint.

'That way,' he snarled. 'The Storm twins lead the way. Keep your eyes peeled boys.'

Caleb knew he had no choice. 'I need a sword to clear a path,' he said, looking at the thick growth of the forest.

Marmaduke nodded. 'Give him a blade,' he told a man standing nearby. 'Something old and blunt. But I'm warning you Caleb. Silas will be right behind your sister and you won't like what he'll do to her if you try anything.'

Caleb glared at Silas, then turned to the crewmate holding out a battered sword and snatched it from him. He walked to the edge of the clearing, took a deep breath and raised his arm, then slashed it down into the thick grass in frustration. He felt the rope go taut around his waist as he stepped further into the forest, mostly pushing the tall grass away to part it but occasionally hacking at it to clear any particularly vicious brambles. He was soon sweating profusely despite the cool shade of the overhead canopy of trees. The thorns scratching at his arms were nothing compared to the limpets on the ship's hull but they still stung and the repetitive movement of the thrashing sword was getting more uncomfortable with every step.

His foot crunched on a layer of dead twigs littering the forest floor. More crackling sounded with his next step. He looked up as he slashed at another thicket ahead of him. The tree above him must have shed a load of branches at some point, Caleb thought. Probably in a hurricane. They were common enough in these parts. His mind wandered to some of the terrifying nights he'd spent on the ship being thrown around like a child's toy. He chuckled as he remembered once –.

'Aaaaaaarhhhhh,' he yelled as his foot disappeared through the brittle branches and he was thrown off balance. The momentum of his body carried him forwards and he fell face first onto the forest floor but he didn't stop there. The matted twigs shattered on contact with his body and he continued to fall past the level of the ground.

Just as quickly he stopped, the rope at his midriff jerking tight as the slack was taken up. His body folded, snapping shut around the rope at his waist, almost causing him to knee himself in the nose. The abrupt halt made him drop his sword which fell silently away into the gloom below. He hung there for a moment, suspended in mid air, then felt a slight bounce and was falling again. He yelped in surprise as the earth swallowed him up, the daylight disappearing above him leaving only darkness below.

Again, he shuddered to a stop. There was a brief pause then he jolted down another small distance, then another. 'Hang on!' he shouted desperately to Eloise. He knew she must have been thrown forwards by the initial fall and he could picture her now trying to support his entire weight as it pulled her towards the pit. If she fell too they were doomed. Everything below Caleb was pitch black and he had no way of telling how deep the hole was.

He juddered down again. Eloise must have skidded closer to the edge. Caleb tried to reach out for the side of the hole, his fingers just able to brush a thick tree root that was poking through the dirt. He heard Eloise shout for help above, then his stomach rose into his throat as a shadow passed over him and he fell once more. He knew in an instant that Eloise had been pulled in after him and they were now both hurtling to the bottom.

Unexpectedly they wrenched to a halt yet again. Silas, thought Caleb instantly. He was closest to Eloise. He'd been holding what was left of the rope. A feeling of dread crept over Caleb as he realised their lives were in Silas's hands. He just had to hope they were worth more alive than dead. Silas wouldn't think twice about letting them fall, unless the captain had told him not to let them out of his sight. He was the last person on Earth Caleb would have chosen to rescue him but everything now depended on the most loathsome man on the ship.

He could hear shouting above, echoing all around him as the sound filled the deep pit. Eloise was yelling, people above were yelling, there was noise and confusion everywhere. Caleb felt himself swaying, the rope cutting into his waist as he hung there helpless. Each time he moved just a fraction closer to the edge and stretched out desperately in the hope he could grasp onto something. His feet hit the wall of the pit behind him and he pushed himself off, digging his fingernails into the loose dirt opposite.

The rope around his waist went slack just as he got hold, his feet swinging down so that he was flattened against the wall of the pit. A split second later Eloise crashed into him, her arm grabbing his neck and yanking his head backwards as she clung on. For a moment he managed to hang on, his fingers clinging to the wall, but then the lump of earth beneath his hands broke away. The side of the pit shot upwards as he and Eloise plummeted into the darkness.

11

Caleb hit the ground with a thump. Eloise landed on top of him a moment later, winding him. He would have screamed out from the pain in his back but he was left gasping for breath and couldn't make a sound.

'Caleb!' came a frantic shout from above. Jasper's voice echoed down the pit, repeating itself a couple more times before it faded away. Eloise put a hand over Caleb's mouth. It was too dark to see her but he understood her instantly. Stay silent and the pirates might assume they'd been killed by the fall.

'Storm!' Marmaduke's voice reverberated around them. 'Storm? Answer goddamned you.'

'Reckon they're squished,' came a Silas's gleeful voice. 'Can't make out the bottom. Shame, would'a liked to have seen that.'

'I'll climb down,' Caleb heard Jasper say. 'Someone get me a rope.'

Caleb swore quietly to himself, willing his friend to

stop talking. He knew Jasper would be desperate to rescue him, just as Caleb would do the same for him, but right now that was the last thing Caleb wanted.

'You'd better be dead, Storm,' called Marmaduke. 'Put that rope away Lorcan. I'm not losing another man to this foolishness. What are the rest of you looking at? Move on, you lily-livered dogs.'

Neither Caleb nor Eloise spoke for several minutes until they were sure the rest of the landing party had gone. Finally Eloise cautiously eased herself off Caleb's aching body and began feeling her way around the floor of the pit.

'Careful,' she told Caleb as he lifted himself up onto his knees. 'There are spikes here. We were lucky to miss them.'

His eyes were slowly starting to adjust to the gloom and half a dozen sharp points gradually came into focus less than an arm's length away. 'What is this place?' he wondered.

'Looks like some sort of natural cave system,' Eloise replied. 'It's too big for anyone to have dug it out. They covered over the opening to turn it into a trap instead.'

'And if anyone got caught they'd end up skewered,' said Caleb, prodding one of the spikes. It splintered easily and fell to the ground. 'These are rotten,' he observed. 'Must have been down here a long time.'

'They would still have done the job if we'd landed on one,' Eloise commented, undoing her bag and taking out the hairbrush Tarian had given her. 'It's only because you managed to push yourself over to the side of the hole that you fell next to them rather than right on top.'

She twisted the handle of the brush to release the knife then cut away the rope from her waist. She handed it to Caleb so he could do the same.

'Now what?' he asked once he was free. He looked at the opening high above them, the rough circle of tree branches with slithers of blue sky breaking through seemingly far out of reach.

'Can you climb?' Eloise asked.

'Only one way to find out,' Caleb answered, hooking his fingers into the dirt on the side of the hole.

'Wait,' Eloise told him. She kicked at another of the wooden spikes poking out of the floor until it was safely flattened. Caleb joined her in clearing the others. If they fell again at least that danger was now neutralised.

'Okay, here goes,' Caleb said. He clawed his way up the crumbling wall until his feet were above Eloise's head. Dirt kept disintegrating around his fingers but he pushed them in deeper to maintain his grip. The surface was uneven enough that his feet were able to find rough ledges to push against, but it was precarious going.

Without warning, a fistful of earth broke away beneath his hand and he fell to the ground with a grunt.

'It's impossible,' he gasped. 'The walls are too unstable.'

'Let me try,' said Eloise, testing the dirt wall with her own fingertips. 'I'm lighter.'

'No, wait,' said Caleb, looking at his sister who was still holding her knife. 'I have a better idea.' He unhooked the clasp of his belt. Pulling the strands apart it separated into what looked in the darkness like a long, single coil of rope. As Tarian had shown him on the ship, one end had a heavy metal hook. Caleb left it on the ground and looked more closely at the clasp on the other end. Pulling it gently with one hand, it bent backwards like a spring under tension. As he let go, the clasp leapt forwards with an eerie twanging sound. 'Remarkable,' Caleb breathed quietly to himself.

'Can it reach?'Eloise asked, picking up the end with the hook.

'We'd better hope so,' Caleb replied, taking it from her and dropping it into the clasp. 'I don't fancy our chances of getting out of here any other way. Stand back.'

He held the belt in the air and bent the flexible clasp down as far as he dared. Too little and it would never make it to the surface. Too much and the clasp might snap leaving them stranded. He took aim at the blue sky beyond a solid looking bough from a large tree that he knew must be standing close to the hole. Caleb took a deep breath, held it steady, then released.

The hook flew through the air, shooting up the vertical tunnel with perfect accuracy. Caleb watched as the thin rope shot after it, past the opening and further on towards the tree. A second later it pierced the lozenge shaped slither of sky above the branch.

'Bulls eye!' Caleb said excitedly as the rope stretched to its full length and nearly tugged the catapult from his hand. The hook at the far end, unable to fly any further, dropped down the other side of the bough. Caleb pulled down and felt the hook bite into the tree. He gave a few more tugs to be sure. 'I'd better go first,' he said, arching his neck back to gaze at the sky. 'Check it's safe. Then I can pull you up.'

'Don't be ridiculous,' Eloise answered. 'You don't need to protect me, brother. I can take care of myself.'

'Very well,' Caleb said, holding the clasp out to her. 'Ladies first.'

Eloise rolled her eyes and took the rope from him. Caleb locked his fingers together to give her a boost but she ignored him and jumped lightly to pull herself up the first couple of handholds. In seconds she was off, scampering up effortlessly, her feet clamped around the rope as she pushed with her thighs, her arms rapidly crossing to gain more and more height. Caleb stood in complete surprise at how fast she scaled the full length of the pit, swinging herself easily onto the forest floor in no time.

'Wait there,' she called down in a loud whisper, wary of making too much noise in case any of the pirates were still close enough to hear. 'I'll make sure the rope's secure.' Caleb picked up his sword and the discarded pieces of rope that had been used to tie them together. He looped them around his chest, figuring they might come in useful at some point. A minute later the dangling belt dropped lower, the clasp now hanging at waist level, as Eloise called down to give him the all clear.

He knew he'd never make the climb look quite as graceful as his sister but racing up ropes on board the ship had been a daily activity for the last two years and he was pleased to emerge above ground at least as quickly as Eloise had. If nothing else it was a sign that his back was recovering well, with no permanent damage to the muscles he'd honed since joining Marmaduke's crew.

Eloise was sitting on the branch above him waiting for Caleb to appear. As soon as his feet were safely on firm soil she unhooked the rope and dropped it down for him to rethread. It took Caleb only a couple of minutes to weave the long coil of leather tubing into a presentable belt again.

'I don't fancy spending the rest of my life stuck on this island,' he said once he was done. 'So I guess we have two options. Get back to the ship, or try to catch up with the others.'

'To join them?' Eloise asked. 'You're not serious?'

'What else can we do? I've no love for the captain, believe me, but we can't get away from here without him.'

Eloise looked at Caleb thoughtfully. 'You know, when I first got taken on board I wasn't completely sure about you. I couldn't tell if you were the same old carefree Caleb I used to know, the brother who was always up to mischief but who I knew without fail would always fight for me. Or had you been brainwashed and would loyally obey Marmaduke like a housetrained puppy?'

'I'm no puppy,' scowled Caleb. 'And you should know me better than that. I'd never choose him over you. Never.'

'I know,' Eloise smiled. 'And that's why I trust you with option three. That map the Duke took from you, it doesn't tell the whole picture. Wade kept talking while you were fetching his water. We don't need the map and we don't need Marmaduke. We're going after the treasure ourselves.'

12

'There's a flaw in this plan you realise,' Caleb called back as he hacked his way through the undergrowth. 'Once we find the treasure how are we supposed to get it off the island without Marmaduke catching us?'

'I haven't figured that bit out yet,' admitted Eloise. 'But we'll think of something.' They'd been walking for half an hour on a different line to the one they'd taken before. The rest of the crew had been following Marmaduke's directions towards the top of one of the island's two peaks but Caleb and Eloise were heading deeper into the lush green valley at its centre. The late afternoon sun had been beating down on them the whole time. Caleb was sweating with the heat and effort of clearing a path and had removed his shirt to tie it around his head as a makeshift scarf. He was covered in dirt and grime from their fall into the pit and now blood was beginning to seep through his bandages where the barely healed wounds were splitting open. Even so, he refused to slow down. Whatever Eloise might think about Marmaduke not having all the information, Caleb knew the captain was a resourceful pirate and he already had a good head start on them.

Despite that, the exertion was starting to take its toll and after swinging his sword into a thicket of brambles he stumbled and fell to one knee.

'Rest a minute,' Eloise told him. 'You're exhausted.'

'I'm fine,' Caleb answered. 'I just need some water. I – can you hear that? What's that noise?'

'I hear it,' Eloise replied. A low rumbling roar was coming from somewhere up ahead. 'We're close. And then I think you'll find what you're looking for.'

'The treasure?' asked Caleb excitedly. He jumped to his feet and began slicing through the greenery with a renewed vigour, wildly beating a fresh path with his sword.

'No,' Eloise admitted as they finally broke free of the rainforest. A stunning freshwater lake was in front of them, fed by a waterfall thundering down from the hills above. 'Water.'

Caleb looked back at her, then shook his head and laughed. Without speaking he ran to the water's edge, throwing his sword and the spare rope to one side before dropping to his knees. Bending over, he scooped the cool, clear water over his face then hungrily gulped down mouthful after mouthful. When he'd had his fill he shuffled comically forwards until he was up to his waist then spread his arms out wide and let himself fall headfirst with a splash. Eloise couldn't help but laugh. Caleb savoured the soothing sensation of being totally immersed, feeling invigorated for the first time in days. He took a few powerful breaststrokes to swim further into the middle of the lake. He could almost feel the dirt washing away and broke the surface again with a big grin.

'Coming in?' he asked Eloise, flicking water towards her.

'Try and stop me,' she said, wading in fully clothed to join him. 'Only keep your voice down, we don't want the others to hear us.'

Caleb looked at the hills above. The crew of The Cutlass were up there somewhere and although it was unlikely they'd be able to see or hear them all the way down here he nodded agreement. Still, he thought to himself, being quiet didn't mean he couldn't have fun. He ducked under the water, swimming across to Eloise and pulling on her feet so she was dragged down. As they both came up for air she splashed water at him then pushed him under. For a moment it was as though they were children again, equally matched twins who were constantly trying to prove themselves against the other, laughing without a care in the world.

Caleb was the first to make his way back to shore, lying down in the sun to dry off. Eloise soon followed, standing over him so that water dripped onto his face.

'Move out the way, you're blocking the sun,' Caleb scolded her.

'No point drying off,' Eloise replied. 'We're not there yet.'

Caleb looked up at her. 'Not where?'

She turned to one side so the waterfall appeared behind her. 'There,' she said, pointing to the foaming water.

Caleb pushed himself onto his elbows. 'We're going in there?'

'That's what Wade said,' Eloise told him, holding out her hand.

Caleb sighed and allowed her to pull him to his feet. Shielding his eyes from the sun with his fingers he squinted at the waterfall on the far side of the lake. The spray was throwing up a perfect rainbow, all seven colours jumping out brilliantly against the white frothy backdrop. 'Did he say how?' Caleb asked dubiously.

'No,' admitted Eloise. 'He just said that if anything happens to the map that there's another path. A short cut. Aim for the lake in the valley below the tallest hill. Go right through the waters of the cataract. Those were his exact words.'

'That's it? That's all he said?'

Eloise thought for a moment. 'Well, it was hard to hear him. He was struggling to get his words out by then. But yes, I'm pretty sure that was all. If there was any more he died before he could tell me.'

'Okay,' said Caleb, picking up his sword and the rope pieces. 'Let's go then.' He pointed to the left hand edge of the falling water. 'That side looks easiest. There's a slight ledge on the rock face. We ought to be able to pick our way across it and get pretty close before we get wet.'

As they set off round the lake Caleb suddenly realised how hungry he was. He ducked into the

79

forest and picked a couple of papaya fruits growing nearby, throwing one to his sister. She caught it gratefully, then walked over to the tree herself and filled her bag with as many as she could fit in. 'Don't know when we'll next see food,' she explained, following Caleb to the start of the rocks.

They clambered over the first couple of boulders but soon came to the wall of rock which separated them from the waterfall. 'This is going to get slippery,' Caleb warned as he reached out to grab a handhold. Testing first that it could take his weight, he then stepped across and jabbed his foot into a fissure in the rock. Slowly, carefully, he worked his way closer to the roaring foam of the waterfall. Glancing back he saw that Eloise was already steadily making progress behind him, methodically placing her hands and feet in the cracks. He knew he didn't have to worry about her. She was as nimble as a mountain goat and would be more than capable of climbing to the very top of the cliff if she had to.

He put Eloise out of his mind as he concentrated on his next move. The spray was hitting his face and arm now and the rock itself was damp to the touch. They weren't high up but one wrong step would send him crashing into the lake. If he landed beneath the full weight of water plunging behind him he'd likely be pounded into the lake bed. At best he'd fall to the side and be forced to swim back and start again. Knowing how easily Eloise would make the climb look he was more embarrassed by the prospect of looking foolish in front of her so focussed intently on each manoeuvre.

Before he knew it he'd made it all the way along

and was hugging the wet rocks with the water thundering at his back. The fine spray had turned into an impenetrable mist that meant it was impossible to see further than his arm. But then he saw it. In a brief gap in the hazy vapour Caleb caught sight of an opening in the rock. He was close, just a few more paces. He lifted his right foot to the next small ledge and transferred his weight to it, ready to bring his left foot closer.

Then he slipped. Years of tumbling water had polished the rock to a slippery sheen and his foot with all of his weight on it slid straight off. He'd already let go with his left hand but still had a tenuous grip with his right. His fingers were white with the pressure of supporting his entire body. He flailed about desperately trying to find something to hold with his other hand, his feet scrabbling at the rock looking for any tiny bit of ledge to latch onto.

With relief his foot scraped against a rough edge. He wedged it in, feeling it bite into the solid wall. His heart was pounding as he flattened his body alongside the rock. If Eloise hadn't been coming up behind him he might have stayed hugging the wall forever but he knew for her sake he had to get moving. Panting heavily, he tentatively stretched out his hand and found the next protruding bit of slippery rock. He grabbed it firmly, cursing himself for being so careless before. No more mistakes, he told himself, as he painstakingly felt around with his leg for a firm footing.

A minute later he reached the dark crevasse and collapsed inside, pushing himself further into the dank tunnel and away from the danger of the water.

Before he'd had a chance to catch his breath Eloise appeared in the opening and dropped lithely onto the wet floor.

'It's pitch black,' she observed as she looked deeper into the tunnel.

Caleb sighed. 'We'll have to go back out to make a torch from the forest,' he said dejectedly. After all that effort the thought of having to go through it again was almost too much. 'May as well have a look round while we're here. You never know, might find something useful.' He stood and edged tentatively into the darkness. With the waterfall blocking out most of the light from outside it very quickly became impossible to see a thing. Eloise put her hand on Caleb's shoulder so they could keep track of each other, then together they made their way deeper and deeper into the tunnel.

'Ow!' Caleb swore as he walked straight into a rock wall. 'It's a dead end.'

'Okay, split up,' said Eloise. 'You feel round to the left, I'll try this side.'

Caleb shivered involuntarily as Eloise lifted her hand from his damp shirt. 'It's cold in here. Are you alright?'

'I'll live,' she murmured as she moved off. Caleb put one hand on the wall and held the other in front of his face to protect him from any more unexpected bumps. It was eerie feeling his way along. The total blackness was disorientating and he began to feel uneasy at the prospect of stumbling into a giant spider's web or a colony of bats.

His foot suddenly kicked a solid stone bar extending out from the wall. He swore quietly, annoyed that he couldn't see a thing. Reaching above his head to check he wasn't about to bump that as well, he stepped onto the stone to get past it. He yelped as it sank into the floor with a low scraping sound.

'What was that?' Eloise asked from the other side of the tunnel.

'Nothing,' Caleb answered hastily. 'Just a rock.' As he said it, a rumbling noise sounded above them, quickly getting louder.

'Nothing?' Eloise shouted above the noise. 'Let's get out of here!'

'I think you're right,' agreed Caleb, hurriedly turning and running towards the light at the tunnel's entrance. 'That's odd,' he said as they neared the halfway point. 'It's brighter out there than it was before.'

At the same time, both twins realised why. The waterfall had disappeared. Where before the sunlight had been blocked by the mist and raging foam crashing past, now there was a clear view out to the blue sky beyond.

'Where's the water gone?' asked Eloise.

At that second the answer appeared behind them. The full force of the waterfall had somehow been diverted and was now thundering into the back of the tunnel. Millions of barrels of water landed on the stony floor, then with nowhere else to go shot down the passage towards them.

13

'Run!' shouted Caleb, but it was too late. The raging torrent scooped them both up and carried them along the rest of the way. A moment later they burst out of the opening and were thrown towards the middle of the lake before landing with a splash. Caleb felt himself being tossed about like a pebble in a whirlpool, then he burst into the open gasping for breath.

Eloise appeared next to him, spluttering and wiping water from her face. They spun round to look at the river that had flushed them out of the tunnel but it was already receding as the original waterfall reappeared. A second later everything was calmly back to how it had been before.

'Did you see that?' they both asked together. Just before the waterfall had regained its full power Caleb had noticed a second entrance.

'There's another tunnel,' Eloise said, still treading water in the lake.

'Remind me,' Caleb said, breathing heavily. 'What were Wade's words again? His exact words?'

'Aim for the lake in the valley below the tallest hill,' replied Eloise.

'And?'

'And go right through the waters of the cataract.'

'Go right,' Caleb said, shaking his head with a rueful smile. 'We went left. We should have come from the other direction.'

'And miss the fun ride?' grinned Eloise. 'Let's do it again.'

Caleb laughed and splashed water at her. 'If that had landed on top of us we'd have been squashed. And who's to say what would happen next time. The water might come in from a different opening. No thanks, I'll wait here ready to catch you.'

'Spoilsport. Right it is then.' She swam to the edge of the lake and climbed out. Her bag was still looped over her body and water was now pouring out of it. 'At lease the fruit's had a good clean.'

Before attempting the climb again they first collected some branches, twigs and a handful of pine cones to assemble makeshift torches. They both knew to pick the fresher green wood rather than old dry bits which would burn too quickly. The pine cones needed to be smeared in tree resin and they took care to get the sticky amber-coloured goo into all the scales of the cones. Next, they split the branches crossways from one end and inserted a pine cone in each to act as a wick. Finally, they wrapped the ends loosely in several layers of large leaves and tied everything tightly with the bits of rope to keep them dry while they navigated the waterfall.

The climb up the rocks was more difficult from this side but Eloise led and they made it to the second opening safely. Caleb wasn't sure if following her footsteps and handholds had helped or that it was simply because he was getting a better feel for the wet rock. Either way, he was happy to step into the cool tunnel and leave the constant spray of the waterfall behind.

While Eloise unwrapped the torches Caleb crouched down and began cracking a flint against a stone with a few pieces of dried grass on. In less than a minute he had a small fire going which he slowly fed with the twigs to build it up. When it was strong enough Eloise held two of the torches to the flame. They caught light easily and cast a warm glow on the damp walls. She thrust the spare branches behind her back into her belt and made sure they were secure. There was no telling how long they'd be in this tunnel and she hoped they'd brought enough.

With the way now lit this tunnel was far less intimidating than the previous one. Caleb still felt a little uneasy, wondering what further traps they might encounter, but at least they had a better chance of seeing them coming. Pirates and smugglers were known to go to extraordinary lengths to protect their riches and whoever had hidden the treasure inside this cave system clearly wasn't going to make it easy for anyone to find it without overcoming the booby traps and challenges they'd set.

'The floor's sloping down,' observed Eloise. 'This tunnel's taking us deeper inside the hill.'

After a few minutes they came to a fork in the passage, the tunnel splitting into two separate openings.

'I think we should stick together,' said Eloise.

'You took the words out of my mouth,' Caleb replied, peering into the gloom. 'Let's stick with Wade's advice I guess. Keep to the right?'

Eloise nodded and they continued making their way along that path. The sides of the tunnel were now dry and dusty, nothing like the dampness they'd had when they'd first entered. Caleb shivered slightly as his wet shirt cooled. He glanced at Eloise to see she had pulled the flaming torch in closer to her own body. The flickering of the two fires cast an eerie glow around them, their shadows dancing on the rough rock walls. The darkness was so complete that the meagre light they were producing barely let them see more than an arm's length in front.

'We must be well underneath the middle of the hillside by now,' she commented as they continued their trek relentlessly downwards. 'If it goes on like this much further we'll be below sea level.'

'I know,' agreed Caleb. 'A moment ago I thought I heard water lapping. Just our ears playing tricks on us.'

'Shh,' said Eloise. 'I hear it too.'

'Do you get the feeling this cave is about to spring another nasty surprise on us?' Caleb asked. He'd never been afraid of the dark before but this was different. Every sense was tingling, as if something in his body was telling him to keep away.

Eloise nodded. 'Do you feel that? There's a slight breeze coming from somewhere. Let's go slowly.'

Caleb took another tentative step forward and jumped as he walked into some creepers hanging from the ceiling. 'Weird,' he muttered, pushing them aside as he continued to inch forwards. He looked up at the ceiling as he moved. 'You wouldn't think these things would grow down here. I wonder —'

He yelped suddenly as the floor disappeared and his foot skidded down the crumbling lip of an enormous hole. He fell and twisted, the torch flying from his hand as he scrambled to grab on to something. Eloise jumped forwards, throwing her own torch to the floor as she grabbed his arms. Caleb's top half was lying on the tunnel floor but his hips and legs were dangling precariously over a big drop. Eloise watched his torch tumble out of sight, the fall through the cold air extinguishing it before it reached the bottom.

Caleb's heart was pounding as she helped him climb back to safety. 'Stupid,' he said to himself. 'I was looking at the vines, not concentrating.' He shook his head in anger at himself. 'Thanks.'

'Now what?' Eloise asked, picking up her torch. She inspected the hole. It stretched to both sides of the passage. 'There's no way of getting round it.'

'I think I can just make out the far side,' Caleb said, staring into the blackness ahead. 'It's too far to jump.' He reached and tugged one of the creepers hanging from the roof of the tunnel. It pulled out of the ceiling, covering him in small stones and dirt. 'Don't fancy swinging across on one of these either.'

'It's a long way back,' Eloise sighed. 'I guess we should have taken the left tunnel.'

Caleb looked up at the creepers. 'This feels correct though. He'd have told you to go left, surely?' He yanked another of the creepers, jumping to the side as it fell to the floor beside him. 'Hang on a sec.' He moved over to the far right hand edge of the hole and reached up. This time when he tugged down hard on the vine it stayed firmly in place.

'Keep right,' Eloise said quietly, echoing Wade's words again. 'Are you sure it's safe?'

'No,' Caleb answered. 'But I don't fancy trying the other tunnel either. This has to be the way to go, I'm positive.' He took a few paces back, put both hands on the creeper and gave it one last pull. 'No worse than boarding an enemy ship, right? Wish me luck.'

Then before Eloise could reply he ran the couple of steps to the edge of the drop and launched himself into the air.

14

The vine took him neatly over the gaping hole and he landed safely on the far side, still holding on tightly. 'Catch,' he called, then let the long creeper swing to Eloise on the other side. 'Can you manage the jump and the torch at the same time?'

'I think so,' Eloise replied. 'Get ready to grab me.' She clenched the vine in one hand, the torch in the other, and walked backwards to give herself the same run up Caleb had taken.

'Keep hold of it when you get across,' Caleb told her. 'We'll need it to get back.'

She gave it a couple of short tugs. Some crumbs of dirt shook loose from the ceiling but the strange rope held fast. Eloise took a few deep breaths and blew them out, then ran and leapt, letting her weight be carried like a giant pendulum.

Her feet touched down softly on the solid floor of the tunnel. Caleb quickly snatched onto her arm but she steadied herself then shook him off. He let go and took the vine from her instead. 'Let's hope that's the last of the traps,' he said as he looped it round a jagged piece of rock sticking out of the wall.

'Look at the positives,' Eloise replied brightly. 'The better protected the treasure is, the less likely it is that someone will have got here before us. Come on, let's go and find it.'

'I like the sound of that,' Caleb agreed as they once again set off down the tunnel. They only had one torch remaining between them now so stayed close together as they walked carefully forwards. After only a short while the passage started sloping upwards, curving slowly to the left as it went.

'I know we must still be deep inside the hillside,' said Eloise, 'but it feels good to be moving higher. I'm worried about the torches though. Let's just light one at a time.'

They crept on, higher and higher, both losing track of time completely. They paused briefly to eat some of the fruit, but whether it was lunch, dinner or a late night snack they couldn't tell. Caleb's torch began to flicker and die and he asked Eloise for a new branch to light.

'This is the last one,' she told him as she held it to the small flame.

The thought of being plunged into darkness made them pick up their pace. Caleb was just about to complain that they were never going to get there when suddenly they arrived. The tunnel ended abruptly and they found themselves walking out into an enormous cavern.

Eloise lifted the torch, the light reflecting off the high walls. They could just make out another passage opening, halfway up the rock face opposite. Other than that there was nothing. No openings, no other paths. And no treasure.

'What a waste of time,' said Caleb, kicking a stone across the dusty floor. It clattered against the far wall and spun to a stop. 'There's no treasure. Or if there was it's long gone.'

'It can't be,' Eloise said, a defeated tone to her voice. 'We can't have gone through all that for nothing.' She slowly swung the torch round again. 'I want to know,' she said. 'Maybe the treasure is gone, someone got here first, but I want to know that we were right at least. See if you can find any sign that it might have been here.'

Caleb shrugged and followed her to one of the sides of the cave. The walls were uneven, the rocks somehow formed over hundreds of thousands of years. High above he could just make out some stalactites hanging from the ceiling, their pointed tips looming ominously over their heads. They worked their way gradually around the space, Caleb getting more and more frustrated as they went.

'There are footprints,' pointed out Eloise a couple of times. 'We're not the first to have come here.' The imprints in the dusty floor were erratic, without moving in any particular direction or giving them any clue where they should go next. When they were about three quarters of the way round Caleb kicked another rock in frustration.

'Ow!' He hopped up and down holding his foot in the air in pain.

'Will you stop messing about,' Eloise told him crossly as she continued exploring the cave.

'It's not me, it was that stupid rock back there. It's stuck down.'

Eloise paused and looked at him, then at the rock. 'Now why would that be, I wonder?' It wasn't much bigger than her hand. She walked over and bent down, holding the flame against the stone so she could look at it more closely. When she gave it a small push it didn't budge. With her free hand she dusted off the grit piled up at its base. 'Look, it's bigger than you'd think. Only part of it's visible above ground and the rest is hidden.'

'Keep the light still,' said Caleb. Planting his feet on either side he leaned down and tried to prise it up with his fingertips. It rose very slightly but then slipped out of his grip and dropped back into place. Adjusting his position, Caleb tried tilting it instead. He put one hand on top of the other and curled his fingers around it then leaned with all his weight, pulling the rock towards him.

Little by little he felt it shifting towards him, then he suddenly fell backwards as it broke free and tumbled onto the floor. Eloise leaned over and gazed into the hole left behind. There was something in there. Reaching down, she took hold of a slim leather folder and pulled it out. Caleb picked himself up and crouched down next to her as she opened it. Inside, perfectly preserved, was another scrap of yellow fabric, virtually identical to the one they'd found in Wade's shoe except for the outline of the island which was more of a J shape this time.

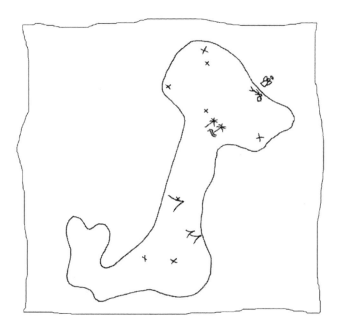

'It's another map,' said Eloise. 'The one Marmaduke has doesn't lead to the treasure. It's a stepping stone to get you to this one. This is the real map.'

'Or another stepping stone,' pointed out Caleb.

'Perhaps,' Eloise admitted. 'But there can't be many. If this one doesn't lead us to the treasure then surely the next one will. Either way, we're now one step ahead of him. We need to – shh, did you hear that?'

Voices were coming from somewhere nearby. Caleb looked up to the other passage which appeared two thirds of the way up the wall of the cavern. A dim light was visible, shimmering from the movement of several torches. The voices were getting louder.

'It's them,' Caleb said. He rolled the rock back into

place. There was no sense letting Marmaduke know they'd discovered anything. The longer he spent searching this place the more time they'd have to escape.

'Come on, quick,' urged Eloise, already at the entrance to the lower tunnel.

'Storm!' came an angry shout from above. Caleb looked up to see Silas standing at the exit of the tunnel, two other men appearing at his side moments later. Caleb gave him a brief wave then darted towards Eloise. A gunshot rang out as he reached the passage, the round smashing off a splinter of rock next to Caleb's head. He glanced back to see Silas brandishing a pistol, a look of hatred on his face.

'You never could hit a thing!' taunted Caleb from below, before he ducked into the tunnel and ran. Eloise was twenty paces ahead of him, her torch lighting the way. 'It won't take them long to get down,' Caleb called as he raced after her. Eloise didn't slow as she raced down the slope. They knew they were safe until the floor levelled out. When that happened it meant they were close to the pit and they'd have to tread more carefully. Until then they could run flat out.

The tunnel gradually curved deeper into the hillside. Eloise was still carrying her heavy bag of papayas and Caleb soon caught up. 'Hold this,' Eloise said, passing him the torch. The flame was starting to dim as the last of the sticky tree resin was used up but there was enough of a glow to illuminate the path. Caleb saw her plucking fruits out of her bag, dropping them behind her as they ran. 'Maybe they'll slip on them,' she panted once the bag was empty.

Suddenly the angle of the floor changed. Running at full pelt meant they'd covered the distance down a lot more rapidly than it had taken them on their cautious walk in the other direction. They both slowed to a hurried walk as the ground flattened out, then crept the last few metres to the hole. Shouts were coming from behind them in the tunnel.

'Quick,' Caleb said, handing Eloise the creeper. 'You go first. Don't argue.'

She nodded and took the vine, swinging across to the far side. Caleb could see the glow from the other torches coming up fast behind them as Eloise tossed the creeper back to him. He caught it just as one of the pirates raced out of the darkness towards him. Without hesitating Caleb ran and threw himself over the hole, the man's hand reaching out to try to grab him as he went. He felt fingers brush his shirt then he was clear. The man emitted a blood-curdling scream as the ground disappeared beneath him and he plummeted into the inky black depths.

As Caleb landed on the other side Silas and another pirate arrived, both skidding to a stop by the hole. The twins didn't wait to see what happened but set off again, running up the passage away from them. Caleb guessed they were working up the courage to follow them, then he heard another echoing scream as one of the men followed the first pirate into the hole.

'Poor guy,' said Eloise. 'He must have tried the jump with one of the other creepers.'

'I hope it was Silas,' Caleb replied.

15

The torch finally burnt out as they were nearing the exit to the tunnel but the faint light seeping past the waterfall was enough to guide them back. Time was of the essence so they didn't even consider climbing carefully around the rocks but instead dove right through the waterfall and into the lake.

'Quick, back to the beach,' said Caleb as they swam to shore. Eloise paused briefly to restock her bag with fruit for the journey while Caleb used the blunt sword to hack a path. They were soon at the edge of the trees overlooking the slender sandy beach.

The only way off the island would be in the wooden pinnace boat they'd used to come to shore. It was small enough that Caleb and Eloise would be able to row it until they were out in the open sea, and simple enough to operate that either of them could then hoist the sail and pilot them to the next island. The good news was by doing that they would leave

Marmaduke and what was left of the boarding party stranded on the island.

The bad news was that The Cutlass was moored right in the middle of the heart-shaped bay, blocking their escape. There were more than enough men still on board to apprehend the two runaways and hold them until Marmaduke could be rescued. Caleb didn't want to think about what would happen to them then.

'There's just that narrow break in the reef,' said Caleb. 'Barely wide enough for the ship to get through. But we have to get past The Cutlass first, and they'll move to block us the second we hit the water.'

'Why?' asked Eloise, grinning meaningfully.

Caleb looked at her then smiled. 'They don't know we're trying to escape.'

'Exactly,' she replied. 'I've a better idea though. I want my sword back and you need a proper weapon too. We'll tell them Marmaduke wants us to meet him on the far side of the island with more supplies. Once we're loaded up then we can make a dash for the opening in the reef. By the time they realise what's going on it will be too late for them to manoeuvre round to block us. Besides, they'll be confused. Where's Marmaduke to tell them what to do? They won't know whether to follow us or wait for him.'

Caleb thought about it. 'They'll wait. Barrowclough will be too nervous about abandoning him on the island. Ready?'

'Then let's go.' Eloise walked confidently onto the beach and together they heaved the little wooden skiff into the gently lapping turquoise water. Caleb was aching all over, blood seeping through his bandages from his many lacerations, but it felt good to be out in the warm sun. He hadn't noticed the pain of his injuries while they were racing back. Adrenaline and the fear of being caught had pushed it from his mind but now as he pulled on the oar he realised how tired he was.

'Take your time,' Eloise said. 'Save your energy for later.' Caleb nodded. They were sitting side by side, each with a single long oar that they were soon rowing in perfect unison, their course set directly for The Cutlass. Once or twice Caleb glanced round to see what was happening on board. Several of the men had come to the edge to watch their approach but no one was making any effort to raise the anchor or to ready the ship.

'They're not sure what to make of us,' confirmed Caleb.

'We'll be fine so long as we get away before Marmaduke makes it to the beach,' Eloise replied.

But there was no sign of any movement on land. Caleb figured they had a head start of at least a couple of hours. After losing two men to the dark abyss even Marmaduke would have been wary of risking more, which meant the long trip back through the hill tunnels. And they would need those hours. He could sail the skiff but he wouldn't be able to outrun The Cutlass for long. The bigger ship, once it was underway with its sails set to the wind, would quickly hunt them down.

'We're coming up on the Cutlass,' warned Eloise.

'Where's the captain?' yelled Barrowclough from

the maindeck.

Caleb waited a couple more pulls on the oar then turned and shouted. 'He's waiting for us. Sent us back to get supplies!' With no further questions from above they kept calmly rowing until they'd passed the figurehead and were level with the main body of the ship.

'Swing her round lad,' Barrowclough called down. 'We'll throw you a line.'

'Wait here,' Caleb told Eloise as he caught the rope. 'I'll grab what I can and pass it down.' With a few strong pulls he scaled the rope and disappeared over the rail onto the deck.

'I need meat and bread,' Caleb called to one of the men standing nearby. 'And the captain's ordered me to collect some items from his quarters. Our swords and a few other bits.

He ran on, surprised at how willingly the crew had apparently believed him. The sooner he could get this done the less chance there was of someone questioning what he was up to.

Reaching the captain's cabin he pulled open the door and disappeared inside, closing it behind him. Both his and Eloise's curved swords were standing in a tall pot just inside the entrance. He was about to grab them and leave but something caught his eye. A collection of maps were laid out on the captain's desk. It was a long shot but if he could find one that looked like the J shape they'd seen on the new map then he might be able to pinpoint its location. He hurriedly rifled through the charts on display but nothing jumped out at him.

The door suddenly opened and Barrowclough

appeared. 'What are you up to Caleb?' he asked.

'The Captain told me to bring him a chart, sir. But I can't find the one he wants.'

'A chart? Where for?'

'I don't know. All he said was it's shaped like a J. Mean anything to you?'

'Aye, of course.' He walked over to the far wall where more charts were piled up in one of the cubbyholes. The second he picked out was the one he was looking for. 'Hook Island,' said the quartermaster as he unrolled the map and spread it out on the desk. He turned it so that the J shape was upright.

'That must be it,' Caleb said, trying to hide his excitement. He desperately wanted to take the scrap of yellowing canvas from his pocket to compare them more closely but he was pretty sure the island Barrowclough was showing him now matched that one exactly. There was a straight ridge of land along the top, the two promontories extending evenly out from the main body of the island. At the bottom the terrain swept round to the left in a large curve.

Barrowclough twisted the island by forty-five degrees to show it in its true position with the hook of the J pointing directly west.

'Safest place to land is here,' said Barrowclough, pointing to the northeast peninsula. 'If I remember right the southwest is littered with submerged rocks so only a fool would attempt to come in that way. The captain will know all that though,' he added, rolling it back up and handing it to Caleb.

Caleb reached out and took the chart but Barrowclough held onto the other end. 'The Duke tell you why he wanted this particular chart?'

'No,' Caleb answered, hoping he didn't look as red-faced as he felt. 'Something to do with that scrap of a map he has. He wouldn't say any more.'

Barrowclough eyed him carefully for a few seconds, then nodded and let go. Caleb moved hastily to the door. He had to leave here now.

'Wait!' called the quartermaster as Caleb was almost through the door. He froze. What had given him away, he wondered, his mind racing. For a moment he debated making a run for it anyway. He could try to get to the skiff before anyone could stop him but there were too many men on deck between him and the smaller boat. He turned slowly to face the ship's second in command.

'Aren't you forgetting something?' Barrowclough pointed to the tall pot next to Caleb. The swords! He'd completely forgotten about them. With the chart in one hand he clumsily collected the two blades and nodded thanks before ducking back out into the open. Men were already passing down a barrel to Eloise. Caleb figured it looked heavy enough to contain enough supplies for ten men. He tucked the two swords in his belt and jumped onto the rail, taking hold of the rope.

'See you soon,' he called as he dropped over the side and quickly descended into the skiff.

'Let's get out of here,' Caleb hissed to his sister. He sat down and took a strong drag on the oar. Eloise matched him and they lurched away from The Cutlass.

'What are you doing you fool. Come about!' shouted Barrowclough when he realised they were heading away from land.

'Sorry Mister Barrowclough,' called Caleb. 'We've an errand to run. The Duke will explain.' He felt a twinge of guilt at the perplexed look on Barrowclough's face. He'd always liked the ship's quartermaster and hoped he wouldn't suffer too much when Marmaduke finally returned. There was no time to worry about that now as they left The Cutlass behind and eased through the narrow channel and out into the rougher waters.

Pulling in the oar, Caleb jumped over his bench to the single mast and raised the mainsail. While he was doing that Eloise moved to the tiller, the simple handle at the back of the vessel which was attached to the rudder and adjusted their course. She aimed directly east in order to lead them out from between the two long tree-lined prongs of the island and into the Caribbean Sea.

'Aim south when we're past the headland,' said Caleb, unfurling a second sail and attaching one corner of it to the front of the boat.

'But there's an island to the north east,' replied Eloise. 'That's much closer, surely?'

'It's where he'll expect us to flee,' Caleb answered. 'I saw a much bigger land mass to the west when I was in the crow's nest. If we skirt round to the back of the island we can make a beeline straight for it. If we're lucky Marmaduke won't even realise where we've gone.'

He glanced behind him, relieved to see no movement from The Cutlass. It appeared their ruse had worked and they now stood a good chance of escaping. For the first time since being reunited with

Eloise he felt like they were finally on top.

'I'm free,' he said quietly as the reality of their situation dawned on him. 'After two years on that ship, I'm free. Free!' he shouted.

'Shhh!' laughed Eloise. 'You'll alert everyone on board. And don't get so excited just yet. We're in a tiny skiff in the middle of the sea with a gang of very angry pirates after us. And all we have to fight them off are two swords and a bag of papayas.'

'Ah, but we do have the next clue to the treasure,' pointed out Caleb.

16

'Cooperstown,' Eloise read as they lowered the sail and rowed the skiff past the entrance to the busy port. The sun had disappeared behind the hills to the west of the town, the sky quickly changing from a beautiful golden pink to an altogether more sinister bluey-grey that very soon would turn to night.

'Ever been here before?' asked Caleb, keen to find somewhere to moor before darkness fell.

She shook her head. 'No. You?'

'The Cutlass came here once or twice but I stayed on the ship. Only the Duke and a handful of men he trusted went ashore.'

'He didn't trust you? And there was me thinking you had a soft spot for him,' commented Eloise.

'He didn't treat me badly,' Caleb admitted. 'Not until you arrived that is. But there was no love lost, believe me. He trained me well but only because he knew his life depended on his crew's ability to fight. It wasn't for my benefit. He certainly didn't trust me enough to let me go free in a town like this.'

'In case you deserted? Would you?'

'I don't know. Maybe, although I'm not sure this place would have been my first choice. It's a pretty lawless town from what I've heard. He'd come here to get supplies and catch up with his pirate cronies, but also to pick up new recruits. Plenty of desperate men to tempt away. It was only once they were out to sea they discovered what he was really like. This will do,' he added as they glided between two larger boats.

The daylight was almost gone as Eloise dropped the anchor over the side. They'd agreed the boat was too heavy for them to pull onto the beach. Even if they could, anything left inside would be stolen within an hour. Leaving it moored in the bay was no guarantee of safety but without men to put on guard it was the only option they had.

'Now what?' asked Eloise, warily eyeing the lights of the town.

'We'll need a bigger boat than this if we're to make it to Hook Island. And a bigger boat means we'll need a crew. Not many, one or two might do, but we can't sail it on our own. That can wait. We can hide out here until morning and get some sleep.'

'Sleep? Are you kidding? With Marmaduke on our tail?'

'You can go and explore the town if you like,' Caleb replied, yawning deeply as he pulled one of the sails over him. 'I doubt Marmaduke will find us tucked in here in the dark. He's a ruthless son of a goatfish but he'll wait until morning to continue the hunt for us.'

'Are you sure?'

'No,' replied Caleb. 'But it's the best we've got and I'm exhausted.'

Within a couple of minutes he was sound asleep. Eloise felt tired but she was also intrigued by the pirate town and wanted to explore it. She put her satchel over her head and tucked her long, red hair under a bandana, then last of all slid her curved sword into her belt. The ornate carved hilt glinted in the dying sun and she stroked it thoughtfully. If there was any trouble she was more than capable of taking care of herself.

She climbed up from the low skiff onto the boat they'd moored next to. There was no sign of anyone onboard. Moving round to the far side she surveyed the bay. Several small boats were passing to and from the larger ships anchored further out in the deeper water. She waited, quietly watching and assessing each one. After ten minutes she spotted what she was after. A stubby eight man craft was ferrying three well dressed men from a merchant ship to shore. She called across as they were passing and they reluctantly consented to giving her a lift to shore.

Night had truly set by the time they reached the main jetty leading into the port. Several fires had been lit on the nearby beach and people were laughing and singing in the darkness. Despite her confidence with her sword Eloise knew it wasn't safe to be out alone. She kept to the shadows as much as possible, skulking furtively around the edge of the harbourside as she tried to avoid any encounters with drunk sailors.

A ragged blanket had been discarded in the

entrance to an alleyway so Eloise picked it up and wrapped it over her head and shoulders. She tried not to think about where it had come from but at least it gave her some protection from the chill of the evening as well as helping to disguise the fact that she was a young woman out alone in a dangerous town.

The wooden buildings along the quayside were mostly bars. The larger stores were down side streets away from the main strip. Eloise knew that ropes, sails, everything they'd need for a long trip at sea would all be available somewhere in the town. If they had the gold to pay for it. How to get the gold, that was their problem. Several messages and adverts had been written on the fence nearby and she walked over to have a look. Maybe they could take on a job to earn some funds, although how they'd ever earn enough to get a bigger boat capable of making the longer sea voyage to Hook Island was a daunting prospect.

Nothing jumped out at her from among the notices. Some were put there by ships looking for crew but since most men couldn't read Eloise didn't imagine the ship owners received many replies. They mostly looked old and faded anyway so unlikely to be of any help to her. One announcement stood out, written in bold black ink on the wooden planks, asking for information on a lost child, Celeste Patrin. One next to it was from someone selling old barrels. None gave her any hope of finding a means of making money quickly.

She jumped as a nearby door crashed open and a man fell backwards through it. He stumbled on the step and slumped to the ground, a bottle rolling from his hand. A loud cheer erupted from inside. Eloise turned and hurried back in the other direction without waiting to see what happened next. The last thing she needed was to get caught up in a bar brawl.

Another door swung open ahead of her, two men staggering out arm in arm. They were clearly drunk as they slurred the words to a well known pirate song.

'Fifteen men on a dead man's chest,' sang the first.

'Yo ho ho and a bottle of rum,' chimed in the second, slamming his bottle against another one the first man was holding. The first took over the song again.

'Drink! And the devil had done for the rest!'

'Yo ho ho and a bottle of rum!' finished the second, as he took a long swig from his bottle. Eloise backed away quietly. They seemed friendly enough but they looked the types that would drag her into singing the ditty with them and that would mean drawing too much attention to herself. She decided she'd seen enough for one night. It seemed the entire town was drunk, or soon would be. It was the perfect time to steal a boat, but not for finding any willing crewmates. She'd head back to the skiff and get some rest and worry about their next move in the morning.

'... will string Caleb up if he finds him.'

'Then he'd better hope the Duke doesn't ...'

Eloise froze. Two men had just walked right past her, their conversation drowned out by the two drunken sailors still singing at the tops of their voices. Even in the dark and seeing them from behind she recognised them immediately. Three days on board

The Cutlass while Caleb was down below recovering from his wounds had given her a chance to get to knew a few of the crew. Jasper and Magnus. Her eyes darted around the crowded dock. If they were here then so were the rest of the crew. Which meant Marmaduke and Silas wouldn't be far away. She'd need to be extra cautious.

She'd known the pirates hunting them were bound to show up sooner or later but they'd been hoping for later. Their unexpected appearance already changed things. It would be far too risky to come into Cooperstown during daylight the next morning. Marmaduke would have his spies everywhere by then. They needed to find a new boat and get away. Tonight.

The two sailors turned a corner and disappeared from sight. Maybe she should follow them, ask if they wanted to join her and Caleb rather than keep serving on Marmaduke's crew. She was pretty sure Jasper was a good friend of Caleb's, but was Magnus? He'd seemed okay the few times she'd seen him but could he be trusted? Even if they chose not to join her, she had to be sure they wouldn't report back.

Eloise knew she had to do something though. She couldn't stay out in the open but she was reluctant to return to the boat empty handed. It would all waste too much time, time they didn't have if Marmaduke was scouring the town for them. The two drunken singers had moved on down to join some others by a fire on the beach leaving the path clear to follow the others. She reached into her bag and took out the hairbrush Tarian had given her, sliding out the knife. The town was getting more and more raucous and she felt safer having it in her hand as she crept to the end of the street and peered round. If she could catch Jasper on his own she was sure he wouldn't inform on them. She just needed to keep track of him until the coast was clear.

Her heart jumped into her mouth. Marmaduke was standing only twenty paces away. He had his back to Eloise but there was no mistaking the imposing figure. He was shouting at Jasper, pointing in a different direction. She knew he must be telling them where to go next to search. The sight of the captain made up her mind. She and Caleb should leave. Right away. They could take their small boat back out to sea and head for a different town on a nearby island. Their survival depended on keeping one step ahead of The Cutlass.

A hand suddenly grabbed her arm and forced her around. She gasped as Silas grinned at her with an evil glint in his eye. 'Wondered who might be spying on the captain,' he leered. 'Reckon he'll be pleased to see you.'

17

Eloise moved without thinking. Her free hand, still holding the knife, whipped up with lightening speed and slashed across Silas's face. He yelped and released her arm in shock, lurching backwards as she thrust it forwards again, stabbing towards his stomach.

The knife missed but the distraction was enough for Eloise. If she stayed and tried to fight then more men would come and she'd soon be overpowered. Her only chance was to run. Marmaduke was just around the corner so she couldn't go that way, but the beach was a dead end so she didn't want to lead Silas there either. Instinctively she dove into the inn next to her, nearly knocking over a red-nosed sailor who was swaying drunkenly inside the doorway. She ducked under his arm, skipped over his outstretched leg and kept running.

A second later she heard a crash behind her. Silas

had come charging into the room and run headlong into the sailor, sending both of them sprawling to the ground. A staircase ahead of her led to some upstairs rooms. Eloise made straight for it while Silas was distracted, taking the steps two at a time.

As she reached the top she risked a glance back. Silas was on his feet but the sailor he'd collided with seized his ankle, pulling him back. She paused to watch the man angrily stand up, holding onto Silas's jacket to support himself. He seemed furious that his drink had been spilled and he wasn't going to let Silas run off easily. She took advantage of the delay and sped off down the corridor. A window was open at the far end. She realised the knife was still in her hand so jammed it into her bag then climbed through. A canopy sloped down to the walkway below. Sliding down it, she pivoted round the bottom edge and lowered herself carefully to ground level.

She wasn't sure if Silas would have followed her up to the first floor or if he was still having trouble with the red-nosed sailor. Or perhaps he'd even come back outside to wait for her. Either way, she needed to get away from this place as quickly and quietly as possible.

Staying under the cover of the canopy she ran lightly to the end of the building and after checking for any unfriendly faces, hurried round. The inns lining the waterfront were all too well lit, with lots of revellers coming and going noisily. The beach was safer. So long as she kept away from the fires she would be hard to spot. She hurried to the short harbour wall and dropped down onto the sand.

The beach curved round, following the natural

contours of the bay. Their boat was moored a couple of hundred metres offshore towards the northern edge. That suited Eloise just fine as there were only a couple of small fires in that direction. The fewer people she might bump into the better.

The edge of the town next to the beach was still brightly lit so Eloise zigzagged down to the water's edge. The sand was damp underfoot but firm and she was grateful the tide was out. Not only did it allow her to put more distance between herself and Silas but it also meant no one else would make a fire this close to the water either. They would know it was only a matter of time before the tide turned and they found themselves having to move. She would have this stretch of beach to herself and so long as she was careful ought to make it safely back to the boat.

Halfway round she heard a groan off to her left in the darkness. She stopped, listening carefully. For a moment she wondered if she'd imagined it but then heard it again. A strange muffled, urgent moan. It was pitch black in this part of the beach and she could barely make anything out. A few large rocks scattered across the sand but little else. She glanced towards the town but immediately realised her mistake. The fires on the beach and the main road destroyed any night vision she'd built up. Turning back to look into the darkness of the beach all she could see was the half remembered image of the flames dancing in front of her eyes.

Treading carefully Eloise edged forward. The moaning had gone quiet but then she kicked something and nearly fell. The stifled noise started again, an earnest pleading tone to it. She gasped as she realised it was a man's leg that she'd stumbled into. She was about to run but something made her pause. The man wasn't moving. Straining her eyes in the darkness, she gradually began to make out his shape, laying spread-eagled on the sand. Ropes were tied to his arms and legs, secured at the other end to the large rocks on the beach. A gag had been forced into his mouth.

This wasn't her problem. Whatever this man had done was his battle to fight, not hers. She knew she shouldn't get involved and took a step away but then a small wave washed up the beach and over her feet. The man let out an anguished whimper. The tide had turned and the ebb and flow of the water was now creeping relentlessly closer.

Eloise sighed. She couldn't leave him here to drown. Whoever had tied him to the rocks may be playing a cruel trick and was planning to come back, but if not then the man was doomed without her help. She looked around the beach one more time. There was no sign of anyone else within a hundred metres.

'If I take that rag out of your mouth, you promise not to shout?' Eloise said to the vague shape in the darkness. It was difficult to see but the response from the man looked like he might be nodding his head and the eager sounds he was making seemed genuine. Part of her was still close to running and leaving him but then she leaned forward to reach for the rag.

The breath caught in her mouth as she suddenly recognised him. 'Barrowclough!' She drew back, more uncertain than ever. The water lapped again at her feet. From where she was standing it was now regularly coming up well past Barrowclough's knees.

'Marmaduke did this to you?' she asked. He nodded in response. 'Because of us?'

Barrowclough hesitated, then nodded again. Eloise shook her head and then before she could change her mind, bent down and pulled the cloth out of his mouth, holding it close in case he screamed for help. He wheezed as he took a huge gulp of breath but didn't call out.

'Thank you,' he rasped.

'I thought you and Marmaduke were friends,' Eloise said uncertainly, half suspecting this to be a trap and for dozens of pirates to jump out at her from the darkness.

'So did I,' Barrowclough replied. 'Eight years.' He spat to one side. 'Eight years I gave that worthless dog. Then one mistake and this is how he repays me.'

Eloise looked at him. A larger swell slid across the sand, drenching his legs and reaching past his waist before it subsided.

'I, uh, hate to rush you Miss Storm but would you mind untying me?'

'So you can capture me and return me to Marmaduke? I don't think so!' exclaimed Eloise.

Barrowclough lifted his head and looked down at his trapped body. 'I don't have much to bargain with. Just trust me when I say I'm not giving that bilge-sucking weasel anything ever again. Especially not you or Caleb.'

'Even after what we did to you?'

Barrowclough gave a small shrug. 'You're pirates. You did what you had to at the time. I'd have done the same. Never felt right what The Duke did to you two.'

Eloise considered him. Freeing him was a risk. A huge risk.

'Tell you what,' he said. 'Just free one of my hands. Please? It'll take me a few minutes to undo the other knots. By then you'll be far away. I won't come after you. I won't even tell anyone I saw you.'

'How about you join us?' The words were out of her mouth before she even realised what she was saying. Another wave washed past, soaking Barrowclough halfway up his back.

'Join you? For what?'

Eloise was reluctant to discuss the treasure of the Emerald Sea, although supposed Barrowclough knew enough already from their trip to Claw Island.

'We're going after the treasure. We have the tender from The Cutlass but need a bigger boat and someone to help us sail her.'

'And to buy a boat you'll need gold,' Barrowclough said.

'Or we could steal one,' suggested Eloise.

Barrowclough shook his head. 'No chance. Owners of ships around here aren't stupid, they'll have guards watching their boats. You won't make it half a league before you have the whole town on top of you. No, what you need is to earn some coin quickly. And I might be able to help you with that.'

'Does that mean you're willing to become a member of our crew?' Eloise asked, watching him carefully.

He lifted his head as a ripple of water washed up the length of his body and, for the first time, reached

past his shoulders, wetting his hair. 'It appears I don't
have much choice do I? You're on missy. I'll join you.'

18

Eloise knew it was a huge gamble setting Barrowclough free but as many pirates said, desperate times need desperate measures. Going in search of her brother in the first place had been a risk. And besides, she couldn't stand there and watch him drown. Taking out her knife she crouched down and cut through the ropes on his ankles, then freed his hands. She wasn't a moment too soon. As Barrowclough stood a wave rolled up the beach right over the spot where he'd been laying.

'Where's your boat?' he asked, rubbing his wrists where the ropes had dug in.

'Out there,' she replied, pointing to the darkness of the bay. 'Can you swim?'

Barrowclough scowled at her. 'I'm a pirate, love.' They walked into the water and both began breast stroking. It was eerie swimming in the inky black waters, the half moon poking out from behind some dark clouds providing little light, but Eloise was grateful the sea was calm in the sheltered cove. It took them ten minutes to reach the small skiff. Barrowclough climbed up first, his years of serving on a pirate ship making it look easy. He leaned down to offer Eloise a hand but she was determined to show she didn't need anyone's help and pulled herself on board. Barrowclough saw Caleb sleeping beneath the sail and grinned at Eloise, holding his finger to his mouth. Stepping stealthily across the bench seat between them, he stood over Caleb and gave him a kick in the side.

Caleb's eyes opened wide and he scrambled back in shock when he saw the pirate looming over him.

'That's for what you did on the Cutlass,' growled Barrowclough.

'Wh-wh-,' Caleb gibbered, confused at the way he'd just been woken and completely taken by surprise at Barrowclough's appearance. 'What are you – ?'

'Doing here?' finished Barrowclough. 'You can thank your sister for that. So Captain Storm, what are your orders?'

'M-my orders?' asked Caleb.

'Not you,' Barrowclough replied, turning to Eloise and giving her a wink. 'A ship can't have two masters. Reckon you're the smart one. What do you say we make way before anyone notices I'm gone, Miss Storm?'

Eloise smiled at him in amusement. 'Weigh the anchor Mister Barrowclough. All hands on deck, ready the oars. What are you doing lying down there Mister Storm. Heave ho.'

Caleb sat there bewildered as he watched

Barrowclough raise the anchor then take a seat at a bench midway along the tiny boat. Eloise did likewise, picking up an oar and slotting it into place then leaning forward and pulling it hard through the water. After three strokes she looked back at Caleb and nodded towards an empty bench.

'Right,' he said, still a bit dazed by the whole conversation. 'Captain,' he added as he picked up his own oar and added his weight to their momentum. They made good progress over the flat water and were soon far out into the bay, where a steady offshore breeze began to create small white-tipped breakers. The rougher water slapped at the pinnace, lifting them and making it harder to row, so Eloise gave the order to bring in the oars and raise the sails. Barrowclough and Caleb worked swiftly and efficiently to prepare the boat for their journey.

'Which course Mister Barrowclough?' asked Eloise. 'You said you knew how we could get some money quickly.'

'Aye, that I did,' said Barrowclough. 'Could be dangerous though.'

'Explain on the way,' Eloise told him.

'Very well. We're going north then.'

Caleb swung the tiller, pointing them directly towards Polaris, the North Star. The sail flapped gently then refilled as the wind caught it and settled, propelling them forwards.

'The administrator of Tortola, Governor Patrin,' Barrowclough continued, jerking his head to the west where a few lights were dimly visible in the distance. 'He has a daughter. Can't remember her name. Doesn't matter. Point is, she's gone missing.'

'Celeste,' Eloise said quietly. The others looked at her, eyebrows raised in curiosity. 'There was a notice in the town,' she explained.

'She could be anywhere,' pointed out Caleb. 'Lost, killed, taken by pirates. It happens.'

'Aye, it happens,' agreed Barrowclough. 'And you'd be right about her being taken. Worth a pretty penny that one. They was thinking to ransom her but Governor Patrin called in the Navy. It all got too hot so the crew went into hiding instead. If they can, they'll sell her to slavers. If not...' He used his finger to mime dragging a knife across his throat.

'What does this have to do with us?' asked Eloise, shuddering at the gesture.

Barrowclough sat back and looked off to the horizon, a clear line where the millions of stars stopped and only blackness remained.

'I know where she is.'

'How?' Eloise asked in surprise.

'That Dutch vessel we captured a week or so back, remember it Caleb?'

'The Vliegende Draeck,' Caleb answered softly. 'The flying dragon,' he translated.

'That's the one. The boatswain, before we sent him to Davy Jones' locker, he told the Captain where she was. Said some two bit smugglers had grabbed her, tried to sell her to Flying Dragon shortly before we crossed paths with then. He attempted to barter for his life by suggesting we rescue her and claim the reward. The fool was forgetting we were pirates. The Governor would have strung us up the second we got within sniffing distance of Tortula.'

'Even if we'd brought him his daughter?' asked

Caleb.

'He'd have assumed we'd taken her in the first place,' Barrowclough said. 'It was too big a risk, for not enough reward. Captain threw the boatswain overboard and that was the end of it.'

'And you think she's still there?' asked Eloise.

'That I can't say. But aye, I reckon there's a fair chance. So long as they've got enough supplies they'll want to keep their heads down. They won't be able to offload her until things have calmed down so my money's on them being holed up. On Cockroach Island.'

*

They sailed through the night, each taking it in turns to man the tiller and keep watch. Caleb felt uneasy while Barrowclough did his shift and held his sister's knife beneath the sail. The arrival of The Cutlass's quartermaster had astonished him and Caleb wasn't completely sure he could trust him. He resolved to stay awake to keep an eye on the older sailor but felt his eyelids growing heavier and heavier as they slowly made their way north.

He woke with a start. The sun was high above , its heat already making life uncomfortable.

'He's alive!' Eloise said mockingly.

Barrowclough grunted. 'It's a miracle either of you are walking at all after what you both went through. I've seen keelhaulings finish stronger men than you. You're a fast healer Master Storm.'

Caleb stretched and sat slowly, his body aching.

The injuries might be mending but he'd been lying in an awkward position all night and felt stiff all over. 'Not fast enough,' he muttered, arching his back and twisting his neck from side to side to loosen up.

Eloise handed him a cup of ale and a lump of dry bread. 'No water?' Caleb asked, pulling a face as he sipped the warm beer.

'This is all they handed us,' she told him. 'And cheese, salted meat, fruit. But no water I'm afraid.'

'Ale lasts longer,' Barrowclough told them. 'Water goes stale too quickly. Rum would have been my first choice. If I'd known I was going to get dragged along on this fool adventure I'd have made sure you were better supplied.'

'At least we've plenty of food,' Caleb replied, helping himself to a sausage and a chunk of cheese. 'And what do you mean, fool adventure? This was your idea.'

'Aye, well, it sounded more feasible last night. Knowing where the girl is and knowing how to grab her, that's a different story.'

'Are you telling me the great Ryker Barrowclough, fearsome pirate, second in command of The Cutlass, scourge of the high seas, doesn't have a plan for how to steal a little girl from a few amateurs? I'm disappointed. What do you think sis, shall we take him back to Cooperstown?'

'I never said I don't have a plan,' growled Barrowclough, glaring at him. 'But you won't like it.'

'Try me,' Caleb replied, holding his stare. 'I'm not afraid if that's what you're thinking.'

'You should be,' Barrowclough warned. 'Fear gives a man an edge. Makes you fight like your life depends on it, which it usually does. You always know when you come up against a man who ain't afraid to die. They're the easiest battles to win. You just,' he added, waving a hand lazily towards the sea, 'help them on their way.'

'Okay, so maybe I am a bit afraid,' admitted Caleb. 'But it won't stop me trying. What's your plan?'

'We trade.'

The twins looked at each other and Caleb laughed. 'Trade? What do we have worth anything? This boat maybe, but we can't give that up.'

'Not the boat,' Barrowclough said. 'You.'

19

The evening sun was low in the sky when Barrowclough pointed to a hazy blot in the distance. 'Cockroach Island.'

'That's it?' asked Eloise. 'It's a rock!'

'There's not much to it,' agreed Barrowclough. 'Which means however scarce a crew they are they'll have men posted at each end. They'll see us coming.'

'Even at night?' asked Caleb, more in hope that anything. He knew the answer already.

Eloise looked at the sky. 'No clouds. It'll be a clear night. It's a waning moon so there won't be much light from that but the stars will be bright enough.'

'We could get lucky,' said Barrowclough. 'If they are there they'll be getting mighty bored by now. Maybe even complacent. No one goes to Cockroach Island for the fun of it. If the Navy haven't found them by now they're not going to. Especially not at night.'

'I still don't like the plan,' said Eloise. 'Handing

over Caleb isn't any help to us.'

'Yeah, well, that's plan B,' Barrowclough replied. They'd been over it a dozen times during the course of the day. If they could sneak onto the island at night there was a chance, a small chance Caleb admitted, that they could take the smugglers by surprise. But if they were seen on their approach the only solution any of them could think of was to offer up Caleb. They'd loosely tie his hands to make out he was their captive then offer to swap. Or better still, hope the other crew suggested the swap. If they thought it was their idea the whole operation would be likely to go more smoothly.

'But what if Caleb can't escape?' asked Eloise for the sixth time that day. 'They might sail off in the other direction and we'll never see them again. I'm not losing him, not after I've only just found him.'

'There are three of us,' Caleb told her. 'We'll be outnumbered, could be ten to one, who knows? And all we have are our two swords and that rusty old blade. We can't fight them. We have to get Celeste away first. When she's clear of the smugglers and safely on board this boat then I can make a run for it.'

'But they'll be watching you!' Eloise insisted. 'They may accept you as a pirate when they hear you're from Marmaduke's crew but they won't trust you. This is stupid.'

'I know,' agreed Caleb. 'But it's the only plan we have.'

They went quiet, both tired of repeating the same arguments. The sun touched the western horizon, the pink and orange sky briefly taking their breath away. The sea was like a blanket of molten lava, gently lapping at the boat as the golden colours reflected off its surface. Then the sun slowly sank, the air turned pale blue and the water suddenly darkened ominously. Barrowclough made sure the tiller was pointing towards the island, keeping it in his sights as long as he could before it faded into the gloom.

'We could get lucky,' he repeated softly.

*

The dark outline of the island rose up before them as they drifted towards the shore. So far they'd seen no sign of life. If the smugglers were still here they must be moored on the far shore, although as Eloise had pointed out, that wasn't particularly far. The island looked like a one-legged man would be able to walk the whole way around in under an hour.

'Plan A,' whispered Barrowclough. It appeared no one had spotted them approaching so they had a chance of taking them by surprise. Caleb had to admit he wasn't disappointed. As much as he'd argued in favour of the strategy to trade him, now they were here he much preferred the alternative plot to capture the girl by stealth.

No one said a word as Barrowclough expertly guided them into a tiny cove on the south side of the island and lowered the sail. They left it prepped to be swiftly hoisted and the oars were ready to be dropped into their clasps in case they needed to make a quick getaway. Caleb gently lifted the anchor into the water then followed it over the side, his sword held above the water as he swam awkwardly to shore.

Eloise and Barrowclough went next. Their belongings were all still on the boat except for a single weapon each. The sea was calm making it an easy swim and they soon regrouped once they were all on land. Quietly they made their way to the rocky outcrop at the back of the narrow beach. They knew they had to be careful not to clink a blade against the stone or to accidentally kick a small rock and send it clattering. Absolute silence was crucial if they were to successfully sneak up on the smugglers.

At the top of the rocks they paused to catch their breath. It was hard to see much at night. A thin layer of grass, punctuated by the occasional large shrub, filled their view. There were no obvious trees on the island, just the thick barren scrubland desperately trying to eke out an existence on the rocky terrain.

They all froze at the sound of laughter came from the darkness ahead. Caleb put his finger to his lips but immediately realised it was a wasted gesture. The others knew what they were doing. Slowly they crept forward, keeping as low as possible as they cautiously pushed through the thin grass. After a short distance they reached a lip and were able to look down on the scene below.

The island appeared to have a natural depression, a crater in the middle protecting the inhabitants from the outside world. They'd lit a fire, safe in the knowledge no passing ships would see the flames.

'I can only see three,' whispered Caleb. 'And the girl.'

'Same,' agreed Eloise. The men were seated around the fire, each holding a tankard. Caleb guessed the nearby barrel was filled with ale or rum. The young girl was sitting closest to the flames. She didn't appear to be tied up but then, why would she be. All three of them knew there was nowhere for her to escape to.

'If we wait they'll probably fall asleep soon,' suggested Caleb.

'Aye,' said Barrowclough softly. 'Or they might decide to leave the comfort of their fire and head back to their boat for the night.'

'Taking Celeste with them,' murmured Eloise.

'That's what I'd do,' agreed Barrowclough. 'They probably give her the run of the island during the day but they'll want to keep her close by at night.'

'What do you think?' asked Caleb. 'Three of us, three of them. Seems like fair odds.'

Barrowclough eyed them both. 'You've neither of you killed a man before, have you?'

Caleb hesitated. 'No,' he admitted finally.

'You can't hesitate,' Barrowclough told them. 'If you freeze, you're dead.' He watched the scene by the fire for a moment. 'We'll spread out, get behind them then move in at the same time. If one of us attacks early it'll blow the surprise for the others. I'd better take the big one with the beard, looks like he might be in charge.'

'Could we find a branch?' Eloise asked, a hint of doubt in her voice. 'Hit them over the head instead? I'll fight a man in combat, it's him or me then. But this will mean sneaking up on a stranger and killing them in cold blood. It feels wrong.'

'They've kidnapped a small girl,' Barrowclough reminded her. 'If the navy catch them they'll be hung.

They've made their choice. And besides, do you see many branches lying around here?'

'I'm with Eloise,' said Caleb. 'We don't know these people.'

'Only kill people you know do you?' Barrowclough asked sarcastically. 'You're pirates for God's sake. This is what we do.'

'No,' Eloise insisted. 'I'm the captain, remember. We give them a chance to release her without a fight. If they resist that's their choice, you can do what you want with them. Can you get to the big guy without anyone seeing you? And hold your sword to his throat? Threatening them may be enough.'

Barrowclough shook his head. 'This has disaster written all over it,' he muttered. 'Fine, we'll ask them nicely. When they say no, then we kill them, happy?'

Eloise nodded, then they all backed away and split up, spreading out in the darkness as they crept around the crater until they were each behind one of the men. Caleb realised he had no way of telling when the others were in position but that didn't matter. Barrowclough would be making the first move and he and Eloise needed to be ready to react. He watched the group intently, particularly the largest of the three who was now sitting off to Caleb's right. The girl was sitting quietly, poking a stick into the flames. The others were ignoring her completely.

Just when he was beginning to wonder if something had gone wrong he saw a sudden movement, the flash of the fire reflecting off a blade, and Barrowclough's sword was at the bearded man's throat. Caleb sprang forward, arriving behind his man at the same time Eloise appeared at the rear of hers. The girl gasped and dropped her stick, looking around her in a panic. All three smugglers were calmer but had clearly been caught off guard. The one being held by Barrowclough didn't dare move but one of the other men made it to his feet, his sword drawn. Caleb noticed he had a tricorne on the floor beside him, the distinct three-cornered hat popular with sailors. It had a large, flamboyant blue feather attached to one side. In the light of the fire his long, expensive coat along with the ornate captain's hat made it obvious he was in charge, but when Eloise touched the point of her own curved cutlass into his back he knew the game was up and dropped his weapon to the ground.

'Evening lads,' Barrowclough said cheerily. 'Just the three of you is it?'

The three men looked at each other. 'Who are you?' asked the one in front of Eloise in a strong Dutch accent.

'Ah, well now,' said Barrowclough. 'That's up to you. I'm either the man who will let you go quietly on with your lives, after I've relieved you of the burden of that young lady over there of course, or I'm your worst nightmare. Which is it to be?'

'You want the girl?' asked Eloise's prisoner. 'We were just debating whether to kill her and move on.' He gave a small shrug. 'You want her, she's yours.'

'That easy?' asked Caleb. 'What's the catch?'

The man looked over to Caleb and grinned. 'I've no quarrel with you, friend.' He stepped casually to his side, away from Eloise's blade, and sat back down. His own sword was still lying on the sand but he gave the impression he didn't care in the slightest. 'Stay for some rum if you want. Plenty to go around.'

No one moved for a moment. 'Thanks,' Barrowclough said eventually. 'But we'll just take the girl and be on our way.' He kept his sword at the large man's throat while he jerked his head indicating Eloise should collect Celeste. She edged closer to the fire and held out her hand to the girl who hesitated, then took it and stood up. Celeste pulled her in closer, as if she was trying to say something.

'There's more,' whispered the girl.

'More what?' asked Eloise, but a split second later she realised what Celeste meant. Too late, she heard the scrape of metal as swords appeared out of the darkness and were pressed into Caleb's back.

20

'Took your time,' growled the man now sitting unguarded. He leaned forward and picked up his own sword from the sand.

'Sorry captain,' came a voice from behind Caleb. 'Thought it best to hold off until you were clear. Plus we didn't want to make that one jump and accidentally cut Hendrick's head off.' He nodded toward Barrowclough who still had the larger man captive.

'It'll take more than a blunt blade like this,' the big man replied scornfully. Caleb couldn't help but be impressed. He knew the sword was old and battered but even so, the smuggler was acting pretty cool considering he had a weapon held to his throat.

'So, it appears we have a stand-off,' said the man they'd called captain. 'Five of us, three of you. Don't much fancy your chances.'

'Oh, I don't know,' replied Caleb. He dove to his right, away from the two men behind him. Rolling over, he let his momentum carry him back up to a crouched stance with his sword raised. 'Seems pretty fair to me.'

'How about a trade?' Barrowclough suggested, trying to diffuse the situation. 'We'll take the girl. You can have young Caleb here. He's a good fighter. He'll be an asset to your crew.'

The man surveyed Caleb critically before spitting to one side. 'I think not. We've too many mouths to feed already. Got any rum? You can have the girl for a couple of barrels.'

'No rum,' Barrowclough answered. 'More's the pity.'

'Looks like we have no deal then,' the man said calmly. He was still sitting but lifted his blade a notch and inspected it as it glinted in the firelight. Eloise pushed Celeste behind her so that she was between her and the captain then raised her own sword. Her eyes flitted to the three men closer to Caleb. The one who'd been sitting by the fire grinned and stood up, slowly drawing his own weapon from its scabbard. They began to spread out slightly but didn't advance. All eight of them held their ground, tension visible in every muscle and tiny movement, their eyes all darting from one to the next as they each sized up the opposition.

Suddenly the big smuggler threw himself backwards, his full weight aimed at Barrowclough who deftly jumped out of reach. He flicked his sword as he did so but missed the man's throat by a hair's breadth, the edge of the blade slicing off a corner of beard and nicking the man's chin. He landed with a crash but rolled and brought himself up to his full height. Caleb gasped. The man was even bigger than he'd looked, his imposing figure now looming a full head taller than Barrowclough who was a sizeable man himself.

Caleb didn't have time to watch any more as the three men closest to him all moved in. The one directly in front of him was the man who'd been sitting by the fire and had felt Caleb's sword in his spine. The others drifted to each side, flanking the first, all three with their weapons raised. Caleb parried a thrust from the middle man then swept his sword back to block a cut from the one on his right, instantly spinning the blade to stop a lunge from the third. The blades all clattered in quick succession as Caleb furiously twisted from side to side, ducking and blocking in a blur.

Meanwhile the captain had leapt to his feet and sprung towards Eloise. 'Keep behind me,' she told the young girl as she brought her curved cutlass down on the captain's sword. The two blades met with an almighty clang that sent numbing reverberations up Eloise's arm but she ignored the feeling and swept her sword round again. She almost sliced open the belly of the captain who barely managed to dodge it, bringing his own sword up in a vicious backhand. Eloise ducked beneath it, the whooshing sound as it passed her ear letting her know how close it had come.

Barrowclough stabbed forwards with his sword but the giant of a man swatted the blade aside with his arm and swung a huge fist at Barrowclough's head. He sidestepped and the knuckles glanced off his temple but the blow was still heavy enough to make him stumble. If the massive fist had connected properly Barrowclough would have been knocked out and he just managed to scramble away from a clubbing roundhouse which whipped through the air in front of his nose.

Caleb hastily arched his back, leaning away from a clumsy but potentially lethal slash from one of his opponents, then rolled to his left to avoid a downwards slice from the man next to him. As he rolled he scooped up a handful of sand and desperately flung it into the face of the third man who'd been about to hack straight at his head. The man staggered and turned, his free hand rubbing painfully at his eyes. Caleb saw his chance and struck, cutting a deep gash in the man's calf. He screamed and fell to the floor. The other two instantly jumped across to protect him and Caleb was forced backwards by their frenzied attack.

The captain of the smuggler crew was laughing as he goaded Eloise, who gripped her curved cutlass lightly in one hand and held Celeste at her back with the other. Behind them was the fire. The captain seemed content to toy with them, feinting left and right and only throwing the occasional thrust in her direction. 'You've nowhere to run missy,' he taunted. 'Swordplay is no place for a girlie. Drop your weapon and maybe I'll let you live.'

Eloise's face was calm as she parried the few attacks from the captain. From the little she'd seen of him she knew her own skill with the sword far outclassed his. If it weren't for Caleb being outnumbered three to one she'd have been happy to let the smuggler wear himself out with his ineffectual attacks, but for her brother's sake she knew she had to finish this quickly to go to his aid. When the captain urged her to drop her sword she pretended to hesitate, lowering her blade as if in submission. He grinned and lunged forwards thinking her defenceless but at the last moment Eloise flicked her cutlass up to block it, rolling her wrist as she did so to wrench the blade from the captain's hand.

He stared in shock as it flew from his grasp and landed beside the fire. There was no time to take prisoners. Eloise stabbed forwards, the tip of her blade puncturing the smuggler's stomach. He fell backwards, speechless, as Eloise rushed and picked up the fallen sword. Out of the corner of her eye she noticed Barrowclough lose his own blunt weapon as the enormous bearded man grabbed it with both hands and yanked it from his grip. He tossed it to one side disdainfully. Barrowclough landed a huge punch right on the man's face that would have floored most people but on the giant of a man it barely registered.

The tall man seized Barrowclough's shoulder and pulled him in, thumping him hard in the stomach as he neared. Barrowclough gasped and dropped to his knees, retching. The man moved in on him, lifting his fist to land a final blow to Barrowclough's head. Eloise flung the captain's sword, the blade spinning through the air towards him and slicing into his bicep before he could land the punch. She darted round the fire and lifted her own weapon again as the man growled and turned to face her.

On the other side of the clearing Caleb was tiring. The two men were coming at him relentlessly, side by side as they beat him back. His own sword had never moved faster and he was successfully blocking wave after wave of attack, but there was no time to get in a strike of his own. He knew that one tiny mistake would be all it took for them to overwhelm him. He had to make sure it was one of them who slipped up rather than him. The man on his right was quicker, by far better with his sword than his partner. Caleb hoped it would be him who erred first but then the clumsier of the two stumbled in the darkness. Caleb blocked a slash from the other and at the same time threw the whole of his weight into a punch that landed perfectly on the left opponent's nose. He felt the cartilage crunch and saw the lights go out in the man's eyes. He wavered for a moment then collapsed to the ground.

Caleb ducked to avoid another thrust from the only man left standing, snatching up the second man's dropped sword as he did so. He backed out of reach as he caught his breath. 'Just you and me now,' Caleb said, panting. 'Want to surrender?'

The man was angry, fury written all over his face. 'You're a dead man,' he snarled, advancing. Caleb adjusted his stance, two years of Marmaduke's training automatically taking over. He turned his body to the side, reducing the size of the target for the man to aim at, one sword held confidently before him and the other lifted high behind him. The man attacked in a frenzy but his slashes were now wild, the poise he'd shown previously forgotten in his rage. Caleb blocked them easily, alternating both arms as he dazzled his opponent with the speed of his two blades. He watched the man's energy slowly run out as he became more and more exhausted. With a sudden flick of his wrist Caleb knocked the man's sword to one side and swiped down on his hand. The man yelped and let go of his weapon. He backed away in fear but tripped over the other man lying prone on the ground with blood pouring from his broken nose.

With one eye on the three men on the floor in front of him, Caleb cast a quick glance across the area. Barrowclough was on his hands and knees, the huge man next to him with his back turned. Caleb realised with alarm that he was advancing on Eloise but then from nowhere Celeste appeared holding a flaming log from the fire. She jammed it into the man's side, causing him to shriek and fall to one side. At the same time Barrowclough reached for a sword lying in the sand and, still on the ground, slashed it across the back of the man's legs. He shrieked and twisted to see where the blow had come from. Barrowclough lunged forwards and thrust the blade into the huge man's gut, falling on top of him as he did and sending them both to the floor. The man tried to speak but blood was gurgling from his mouth, then he shuddered and lay still.

21

Eloise ran over to Caleb and joined him in ushering the three injured men towards the fire. The fight had gone out of them and they didn't attempt to resist as their remaining weapons were taken.

'We should kill them now,' Barrowclough said. He tried to pull the sword out of the big man's stomach but the suction from his blood and vital organs kept it stuck in place. He put his foot on the man's chest and tugged it free with both hands, the weapon making an oozing slurp as it slid out. He bent over to wipe it clean on the man's shirt then approached the captain. He was still sitting where he'd fallen, both hands clasped to his own gut as he eyed the sword warily.

'Not yet,' said Eloise. 'Tie up the others while I talk to this one. Where's your ship?' she asked, pointing her cutlass at the captain's head.

He looked at Eloise steadily then spat at her feet. The wound in his gut looked bad but there was no blood in his mouth so there was a good chance it wasn't fatal. She could soon change that though.

'Okay,' Eloise said matter-of-factly. 'Kill him.'

Barrowclough handed the piece of rope he'd found to Caleb then stepped forwards. He drew his new sword, ready to drive it into the captain's chest.

'Wait,' he said at the last second. He stared at the sharp tip of his own blade then turned his gaze to Eloise. 'A man shouldn't be killed by his own sword, it'll bring bad luck in the afterlife. It's on the north shore.'

Caleb gave his sister a small shrug. He hadn't heard that one but knew sailors could be a superstitious bunch and it sounded believable enough. Barrowclough snorted then went back to binding the other men while Eloise continued her interrogation.

'Anyone else on board?'

The captain hesitated then nodded. 'One. A slave left to guard the ship.'

This time it was Eloise's turn to spit at the captain's feet. 'Slavers,' she said with disgust. 'But you trust him not to sail away?'

He paused before replying. 'He's chained to the deck. If there was any sign of trouble he was to call for help.'

'His name?' asked Eloise.

'Yaro,' the captain replied sullenly.

'Weapons?' enquired Caleb, but received just a shake of the head in reply

'What were your plans for the girl?' Eloise asked, glancing behind her to check Celeste was safe. The young girl was standing to one side of the fire. She was still holding the log she'd used to burn the large bearded smuggler. Eloise couldn't tell if she wanted it close for her own protection or, from the venomous look in her eyes, whether she was contemplating using it on the rest of her captors.

The captain shrugged. 'Lie low until they stopped searching for us then sell her to the highest bidder.'

Eloise considered the four men in turn. They were smugglers who'd kidnapped the young daughter of the governor. By any court in the land they'd be sentenced to death by hanging. She knew she ought to secure the prisoners and deliver them to the authorities along with Celeste. She also knew that would be risky. For one thing they were still outnumbered and a lot of things could go wrong once they were at sea. For another, Barrowclough and Caleb were pirates themselves. Not only was is unsafe for them to show their faces in Tortola, they were in equal danger of other pirates hearing about it. There wasn't much honour among thieves but surrendering these men to Governor Patrin was guaranteed to earn them a black spot, a death threat among pirates.

'We're taking your ship,' she decided. 'And freeing Yaro. I hope you treated him well because I'm going to let him decide your fates.'

'We should kill them now,' growled Barrowclough.

'If that's what Yaro wants then so be it,' Eloise told him. She leant down and picked up the tricorne hat from the sand, placing it firmly on her own head. 'I rather like this. Now, tie this scurvy-ridden waste of space up with the others.'

Caleb stepped forward and grabbed the captain's

shoulder, pulling him roughly to his feet. 'He's got your sword,' he said, pointing to Barrowclough. 'And she's got your hat. I'm feeling a bit left out.' He looked the man up and down. 'Lose the coat.'

The captain glared at him, then shrugged off the long blue coat. He had to switch the hand pressing tightly into his belly before dropping it off his other arm onto the floor. 'Careful,' warned Caleb with a smile. 'Don't want to spill any more blood on it now, do we?'

He picked it up, keeping a watchful eye on the incensed smuggler as he did so. For a moment he thought the captain might kick out at him and Caleb was ready to dodge the attack, but he simply looked down at Caleb scornfully then walked over to his companions. He sat down gingerly, the wound clearly causing him a lot of discomfort, and let Barrowclough bind him to the others without putting up any resistance.

'Be seeing you,' he said, his eyes still firmly on Caleb. Eloise wondered if she'd made the right decision about letting the men live and a large part of her hoped Yaro would do the job for them.

'Come on,' she said instead, taking Celeste's hand. The young girl gave the four captives one last look then threw the flaming log on the sand and turned her back, allowing Eloise to lead her into the darkness.

It only took a few minutes to reach the beach on the north of the island. The night was clear with a million pinpricks of light in the black sky, but even so with its sails dropped the smugglers' ship was barely visible. It appeared to have been painted a deep grey and if it hadn't been so close to shore Eloise wasn't sure they ever would have seen it. A small rowing craft was pulled up on the sand. She helped Celeste into it then the three of them pushed it into the water and rowed the short distance to the boat.

'The Unicorn,' Caleb said softly as he saw the name emblazoned on the stern. 'Suits it,' he added as they got closer. The long bowsprit sticking out of the prow was twisted just like a single horn. The dark silhouette loomed over them but all around them was silence. Caleb wondered if the slave was asleep but then a loud squawk shattered the peace. 'Aar! Who goes there? Who goes there?' The strange noise was quickly followed by a deep voice above them.

'That you captain?'

They didn't answer until they'd drawn alongside and climbed on board. A single man was standing before them, his clothes ragged and his feet bare. Caleb couldn't be sure how old the man was. His head was shaved so that he was completely bald and although his dark complexion had a youthful quality there were deep creases spreading out from the corners of his eyes.

'You must be Yaro,' said Eloise, standing directly in front of him with her companions on either side.

'Aar! Yaro, Yaro,' came the squawking noise again. Caleb glanced past the man facing them to see a cage with a bright green parrot moving about inside. He let out a surprised snort, amusement in his eyes at the funny looking bird.

'You're a free man now,' Eloise continued, ignoring the bird. 'But you're welcome to stay on our crew until we reach Tortola.'

Yaro looked at her, then his mouth split to reveal an enormous grin. He started chortling, the sound rapidly developing into a huge belly laugh. Caleb immediately saw where the lines around his eyes had come from and couldn't help grinning with him. This man was no stranger to smiling.

'Captain de Hoen is dead?' Yaro asked, then burst into another fit of laughter.

'Aar! Dead. Dead,' chirped the parrot.

'Not yet,' Eloise admitted when he'd calmed down enough to hear her. 'They're to undergo a fair trial by jury first.'

Yaro had been bent double, his hands on his knees, but he suddenly stopped laughing and looked at her seriously. 'Who's on the jury?' he asked.

'Just you,' Eloise replied, a glint in her own eye as Yaro's booming laugh returned. Yaro's mirth was infectious. 'The big one is dead,' she told him. 'And the captain is injured. They're tied up by the fire.'

Yaro nodded and looked back towards the dark shadow of the rocky island. 'Not much growing here,' he told them. 'Some dry patches of grass, a few thorny bushes. Nothing edible. They've practically starved me the last six months. I say we leave them here, see how they like it.'

'Very well,' Eloise nodded. 'And are you willing to join our crew? Until Tortola.'

'Until Tortola,' agreed Yaro.

22

It didn't take long for them to realise their new ship was fast. Very fast. The two-masted sloop was perfectly streamlined and with no cargo they sat high in the water. The prow was carving through the sea at a speed Caleb had never before experienced. The tender being towed behind was bouncing over the waves but again, with no weight on board it wasn't adding any drag and so long as the rope held it looked in good shape to stay with them.

Although larger than their tender The Unicorn was still small enough that the four of them could just about handle it. Yaro explained how they'd previously had a crew of twenty men. Captain de Hoen had left the rest of the men in port on Crab Island over twenty-five leagues away. The kidnapping of Celeste had been a hasty and ill-thought through undertaking, a spur of the moment decision when the captain had stumbled on an opportunity to take her. When things had gone wrong they didn't have the manpower to fight so had been forced to go into hiding.

'Aar!' squawked the parrot. 'Hiding, hiding.'

'Clever bird,' Caleb commented, peering into the cage and putting a finger through the bars. The parrot immediately ducked its head and pecked it. 'Ow!' Caleb exclaimed, quickly pulling it away. He put his fingertip in his mouth to suck the blood that had appeared.

'Wouldn't do that if I were you,' Yaro grinned. 'That thing's even crazier than we are.'

Caleb glared at the parrot. 'What's with all the aars?'

Yaro shrugged. 'We figured she thinks that's her name. The crew called her Archimedes.'

'Well, good night Archimedes,' Caleb said, gently tapping the cage. 'Wake us at sunrise would you?'

'Aar! Sunrise. Sunrise!'

Barrowclough took the helm, allowing Eloise and Caleb to grab a few hours sleep but they were soon up again and were debating what to do about Celeste. The original plan had been to rescue her then use the reward to lease a bigger boat but they now found themselves already in possession of a fast ship. Celeste had become an inconvenience, although her cheerful presence on board meant that none of them minded. She and Yaro had particularly hit it off, the large ex-slave constantly joking with her as he taught her how to carry out the vital chores on board.

'We should return her to her father,' insisted Eloise. She was sitting on the main deck with her brother, the ornate captain's hat still perched jauntily on her head.

'And what if he arrests us?' asked Caleb, who'd removed the long blue coat and bunched it up against the foc'sle so he could rest more easily against it. The wounds on his back were stinging and the coat eased the pressure. He'd initially felt pleased that the swordfight on cockroach island hadn't caused him any discomfort but as the adrenaline had worn off he'd become aware that his entire body ached. A couple of days rest at sea couldn't have come at a better time.

'We have his daughter,' Eloise pointed out. 'She'll be able to explain how we rescued her.'

'You think a man like that listens to a child? And if he knows it was this ship that took her he'll hang us first then ask questions later. At the very least he'll detain us until he's satisfied. It will cost us days. We can't afford to wait.'

'The treasure has been there for thirty years,' pointed out Eloise. 'Another few days won't make any difference.'

'Ooh, is there treasure?' asked a small voice above them. Caleb and Eloise looked up sharply to see Celeste looking down at them. She was lying on the foredeck, her head resting on her hand as she peered over the edge.

'How long have you been there?' asked Eloise.

'A while,' admitted Celeste. 'And Caleb's right. Father won't listen to me. He'll lock you up and say he's caught the people who took me rather than pay out any reward. He never pays anyone if he can help it.'

Caleb looked at his sister with an 'I told you so' look. Eloise frowned at him then turned to Celeste. 'Is there anyone else you want to go to? Somewhere you'd be safe?'

The young girl thought for a moment. 'I feel safe with you,' she finally replied.

Eloise sighed and looked towards the rear of the ship. Barrowclough was at the helm, steering them northwest while ordering Yaro to adjust the large grey mainsail. They were a perilously small crew. If they encountered any trouble she was worried they'd never be able to protect her.

'It might seem that way now,' Eloise explained. 'But things can get dangerous very quickly at sea.'

'I know,' Celeste replied matter-of-factly. 'That's why we shouldn't wait any longer. We can go and get the treasure now. I can come with you.'

'She's wise for her age,' Caleb said, amused at Celeste's logic.

'She's too young to be at sea,' Eloise replied. 'She's just a child.'

'I'm not a child,' the girl replied. 'I'm nine and a half! I can take care of myself.'

Caleb grinned. 'We were pretty independent at that age, remember?'

'That was different,' Eloise said. 'We had each other. And dad had trained us how to use a sword.'

'Then we'll train her,' urged Caleb. 'We'll teach her weapons, sailing, how to cook, how to sew –'

'I can sew,' called down Celeste.

'There you go,' Caleb said. 'She's practically a sailor already. Come on El. Hook Island, the treasure. Let's go and get it. All four and a half of us.'

Eloise glared at him but couldn't prevent herself letting out a small laugh at his last comment. 'Mister

Barrowclough?' she called to the back of the ship. 'How long to Hook Island?'

'With a fair wind,' he pondered, looking at the empty sea stretching out before them. 'A day? Maybe two.'

She shook her head and let out an exasperated sigh. 'Very well Mister Barrowclough. Set your course. Hook Island it is.'

*

The day passed quickly. The baking sun sapped their energy and drove them all to seek shelter in the shade of the large grey sail. Yaro told them how the ship's colour was designed to help them blend into the background. Whether it was day or night the smugglers had preferred to be as invisible as possible, relying on their speed and camouflage to avoid being caught rather than having to fight.

At around noon Caleb removed his shirt, causing Yaro to wince at the sight of the raw wounds on his back. He lifted his own top to display a similar sight. Four years as a slave on various vessels had meant many beatings and he spoke of how he'd felt the wrong end of the lash more than once. The two formed an instant bond over their experiences and any lingering doubts Caleb may have had about Yaro's loyalty were soon forgotten.

Celeste kept herself busy running errands all over the ship. She darted about, fetching an apple for Barrowclough or racing up the mainmast to act as lookout. The sloop had no crow's nest but the two masts could be climbed quickly enough, with footholds to allow Celeste to stand comfortably. Any free time she had was spent trying to teach Archimedes her name but for once the parrot was proving unusually stubborn.

Eloise spent most of the day studying the scrap of map they'd discovered in the cavern on Claw Island. The shape exactly matched the chart of Hook Island Caleb had stolen from The Cutlass. Barrowclough described the terrain to her, as best as he could remember. The island was uninhabited but it was occasionally used for shelter in a storm or to replenish fruit and fresh water supplies.

'As I told your brother,' he said, pointing to the chart. 'When he was hornswaggling me back on The Cutlass.' He shot Caleb a mock scowl making Eloise smile. She knew all was forgiven for the way Caleb had cheated him on The Cutlass but that wouldn't stop Barrowclough grumbling about it whenever he got the chance. 'The sheltered waters in the hook of the J is where most first-timers would attempt to land. That will be the last mistake they'll make. It's a ship graveyard. Lethal jagged rocks hidden just below the surface.'

'So we come in from the east?' asked Eloise.

Barrowclough shook his head. 'None too friendly that side either. No, the only safe harbour is the northern shore. We'll need to skirt round the island and come in that way.'

They took shifts during the night, managing to keep up a good pace, and it was early the next morning when Celeste called down from the top of the mast that she could see land. Barrowclough lifted a telescope to his eye to study the hazy mass sitting on the horizon.

'There she is,' he said with a satisfied air. 'Dead ahead. Not bad even if I do say so myself.'

With the speed The Unicorn was travelling the island soon grew in front of them. They were approaching directly from the south so it was hard to make out the true shape of the land, although Caleb could see the far northeast promontory jutting out to the right of the curve of cliff before them.

'The sea looks very calm on the west coast,' he observed. 'You sure we can't head in from there?'

'Don't let it fool you,' warned Barrowclough. 'And you can see how it churns up on the east side. It's going to get bumpy while we pass but we'll be fine once we round the headland.

Barrowclough proved to be understating the conditions as they ploughed through the waves along the coastline. Celeste turned green and spent the time with her head hanging over the side. Anything which wasn't firmly tied down crashed around them and it was only Yaro and Caleb's years spent at sea which kept them from being thrown overboard while they hurried to lower the sails and try to slow the ship.

Eloise stood on the upper deck behind Barrowclough, holding on grimly to the rail as she watched the northeast arm of Hook Island approach. The prow repeatedly lifted high in the water on the crest of each wave before falling steeply into the next trough leaving her with the feeling that her stomach was still floating somewhere high up on the last swell. Finally the turn approached. Barrowclough shouted orders to Yaro to drop the mainsail fully to kill their speed so that he could bring them to a gentle stop on the northern shore.

The cliff swept by on their left, Barrowclough clinging on firmly to the tiller as they approached the calmer water beyond. A few seconds before they reached the turn he pushed it fully away from him, forcing the rudder through the water and swinging them round perfectly to come to a stop. The smaller sails flapped loudly, protesting at the sudden change in wind direction, then filled again and slowly began to pull them forwards along the northern coastline. But that was the last thing Barrowclough or any of them wanted. Too late, they realised a ship was moored in front of them, its cannons all lined up and ready to fire. The Cutlass had beaten them to it.

23

Caleb and Eloise jumped onto the rail, each with one hand on the rigging to steady themselves as they faced the Cutlass with only a narrow channel of sea between them. There was no chance of outrunning the larger ship before it opened fire. They were practically at a standstill and were now a sitting duck. Their only hope was to talk their way out of it.

'You found us then,' Caleb called across, spotting the Duke on the upper deck.

'Master Storm,' Marmaduke answered, turning to look at them. 'Or should I call you Captain Storm now I see you've gained yourself a new ship?'

'How did you know where to come?' Eloise asked, totally thrown by the reappearance of The Cutlass. The pirates' presence here made no sense at all. The last time she'd seen them had been on Cooperstown when Silas had nearly managed to capture her. There was no way they could have known to come here.

'Your brother should have stolen more of my

charts to hide your true destination,' Marmaduke explained. 'When the crew told me young Caleb left with food, weapons and one of my maps it didn't take me long to work out which one was missing.'

Caleb groaned and shook his head. Such a stupid mistake. He might as well have painted the name of Hook Island in giant letters on the Jolly Roger before leaving.

'I admire your nerve, Storm,' Marmaduke added. 'First you steal my tender then you have the gall to come back on board and steal my food from that fool Barrowclough. Perhaps we'll make a pirate of you after all.'

'So what happens now?' asked Caleb. He noticed Silas at the front of the ship, his lips curled in an evil leer. He ran a finger across a scar on his cheek then held up a large knife and pointed it at Eloise.

'Now? I was thinking a partnership,' Marmaduke answered, apparently unaware of the threat from Silas. 'I have one map, covered in symbols which make no sense. I believe you've found a second map which has sent you here. I think you need both to find the treasure. And if the rumours are true there's plenty enough to go around. I say a fifty-fifty split, from one captain to another.'

'Don't trust him,' Eloise said in a low voice.

'Of course I don't trust him,' Caleb said. 'But what choice do we have? Whether he's right about the maps or not he has us perfectly in his sights.'

'Caleb's right,' Barrowclough's voice came from behind them. 'He can scuttle us whenever he likes.'

'Give us a minute,' Caleb called back before jumping down onto the deck.

'Take your time,' Marmaduke chuckled. 'We're not going anywhere.'

The five of them on The Unicorn, including Celeste, gathered on the deck. Barrowclough kept one eye on The Cutlass but the pirates didn't appear to be in any rush to do anything. Several of the crew were standing around watching but none looked like they were preparing to board the smaller ship. There was no need to. Marmaduke had them right where he wanted them.

'Do we need the other map?' Caleb asked once they'd all gathered.

Eloise shrugged. 'It's possible.' She took out the plan of Hook Island they'd recovered from the cave and spread it out on the floor in front of them. 'There are strange markings on here too, but Marissa Cortez clearly liked to set traps for anyone who came searching for her treasure. There might be something we still need on that other one.'

Caleb nodded. 'Let's assume we need it. We agree to go ashore on equal terms. Two of us, two of them, right?'

'And what's to stop Marmaduke scuttling The Unicorn the second you're off the ship?' asked Barrowclough. 'No offence but I'm none too keen on sitting here empty-handed with a dozen cannons aimed at my backside.'

'And we wouldn't want you to either,' Eloise assured him. 'For one thing, our crew comes first. For another, we're responsible for Celeste and I'm not leaving her in harm's way. And thirdly, we'll need The Unicorn to escape afterwards. If they sink her we'll be just as dead as you.'

'Okay,' said Caleb. 'So we tell Marmaduke to stand his cannons down. We'll move the ship out of range then use the tender to sail into shore. That will keep you three safe. Fair?'

Barrowclough and Yaro nodded agreement.

'And if anything happens to us, you see to it Celeste gets back safely to Tortola,' Eloise told them.

'Tell me more about the west coast,' Caleb said. 'You said never to head in that way didn't you?'

'Aye, that's right,' said Barrowclough.

'Even at high tide? In a small ship with a shallow draught?'

Barrowclough considered him warily. 'I suppose at high tide it may be possible,' he answered slowly. 'You'd still be a fool to try it though.'

Caleb grinned. 'Well it's lucky we have a fool of a quartermaster in charge of this ship then, isn't it?'

'Just because The Duke says it,' grumbled Barrowclough. 'Doesn't mean I'm crazy enough to do it.'

'But it could be done,' urged Caleb.

Barrowclough sighed then nodded. 'Aye, it could be done.' He looked out across the wide sweep of beach running the length of the northern shore of the island. 'Reckon high tide will be around sunset. You get yourselves to the west by then and we'll be there to pick you up. Otherwise you'll have a long wait overnight until we can get to you in the morning.'

Caleb nodded. 'So, if we find the treasure, we split the bounty and let the two from The Cutlass come back north while we head west. It means we'll only get half the emeralds but it'll give us a good chance of escaping with our lives which is more than we'll get if we try to come this way.'

'And if they follow us?' asked Yaro.

'Then they're even bigger fools than we are,' said Barrowclough. 'A ship that size in those waters? No chance.'

'Does anyone have any better ideas?' asked Caleb. They all shook their heads so Caleb nodded and stood up to shout across to Marmaduke. 'Agreed. Fifty-fifty split. Send two of your men to shore and we'll meet them there. And stow your cannons. I'm moving The Unicorn out of range so I know she's safe while we're away.'

Marmaduke looked amused at the instructions but gave a mock bow of understanding and began ordering his crew to do as Caleb had said. Meanwhile Eloise and Yaro raised their own mainsail to half mast and Barrowclough slowly guided the ship to a safe distance offshore.

'Keep going,' Caleb told him as he and Eloise climbed down to the tender. 'And if you see a single sail go up on The Cutlass you'd better move quickly. He has a full crew on board and it won't take him long to chase you down at this speed.'

'Don't worry about us,' Barrowclough growled. 'This ship's a beauty, we can outrun them. Just make sure you're on the west coast by sundown.' He untied the rope to the tender and cast them off. Caleb raised the single sail and sat back to study the view as Eloise took the tiller and guided them towards the island.

24

Caleb wasn't surprised to see Marmaduke waiting on the sandy beach for them but he had to suppress a feeling of revulsion when he saw he'd brought Silas Cragen with him.

'I said to bring two men, not a weasel,' Caleb spat.

'Now now, master Storm. We're all on the same side. One happy family. Now, which way? And no tricks this time or I promise your ship will be turned into splinters.'

Caleb glared at Silas who just grinned nastily back. Eloise broke the silence first.

'Up there,' she pointed, gazing at the top of the cliff. 'About a third of the way along this beach. The symbol on the map has a man lying down with a circle beneath his head and an angel above him. I think it's referring to the bible. The circle is the stone Jacob laid on when he had his dream about a ladder to heaven.'

Marmaduke nodded. 'You think there's a ship's

Jacob's ladder somewhere on the cliff?' He swept his hand out to usher her on. 'Very well. Ladies first. Silas will stay with you. Your brother and I won't be far behind.'

Eloise wrinkled her nose at Silas then set off walking along the beach alone. Silas smirked then followed.

'It appears your sister inherited all the brains in the family,' commented Marmaduke. He waited until the others were twenty paces ahead then began walking in the same direction. Caleb made sure he stayed close, hoping Eloise knew what she was doing. She'd explained her Jacob's Ladder theory to him the night before but there were a lot of other symbols to consider and she didn't have answers for all of them.

'So tell me Caleb, what will you do with your share of the treasure?' asked Marmaduke casually.

'Do with it?' asked Caleb. 'I, I don't know. I hadn't really thought.'

Marmaduke smiled and looked at him out of the corner of his eye. 'You're out of your depth boy.'

'Well, what will you do then?' asked Caleb.

'Ships,' answered Marmaduke without hesitation. 'Lots and lots of ships. I'll own these waters. A whole fleet, reporting to me. I'll need captains of course. Who knows, if you can't think of anything to spend your portion of the bounty on maybe you'll be drawn back to the sea. You've proved you can be resourceful. I could use a good man like you.'

'Work for you?' Caleb laughed. 'Don't worry, I'll think of something to spend it on.'

Ahead of them they noticed Eloise divert away from the beach and move closer to the cliff. The jagged rock face towered ominously above them.

'There's no ladder here,' said Marmaduke dismissively as he scanned the precipice. 'Perhaps your sister isn't as smart as she thinks she is.'

Eloise, who'd been walking directly next to the cliff, suddenly disappeared in front of them. A moment later so did Silas. Caleb and Marmaduke hurried to catch up. As they reached the spot where the others had gone they realised the craggy rock briefly folded back on itself creating a hidden pocket before the cliff continued on its way.

'Well I'll be blowed,' breathed Marmaduke. On their left, clamped securely to the outcrop of rock, was fastened a chain link ladder.

'Some of these rungs don't look too healthy,' observed Silas, rapping the edge of his sword on one of the wooden struts connecting the two chains. Bits of damp bark crumbled to the floor.

'They're wetter down here by the beach,' Eloise said. 'Should be stronger once we get higher.'

Marmaduke nodded. 'Better watch your step then.'

Eloise moved to the bottom of the ladder and swung her bag round to her back, a grim look of determination on her face. Putting both hands on the chains she lifted her foot onto the first rung and pushed herself up. The rung immediately split, sending her to the ground with a jolt. Undeterred, she reached up again and pulled herself higher, ignoring the rungs and planting her feet firmly on the cliff side as she let the chains take her weight.

Carefully, Eloise began walking up the cliff using the chains as a guide rope. Once she was several metres off the floor she put a tentative foot on the closest rung and cautiously tested it with her weight. The wooden baton felt solid. She twisted her wrists around the chains and gripped them tightly then took another step to the next rung, breathing a deep sigh of relief when it held.

Gradually she increased in confidence as each step took her higher and higher. The ladder shook as Silas hoisted himself past the first dozen rungs then also switched to standing on them. Caleb moved to go next but Marmaduke hauled him back.

'I'll go first,' he growled, then grabbed the chains and began pulling himself up.

'Scurvy dog,' muttered Caleb, waiting until Marmaduke was onto the stronger rungs before following. He was a little nervous that four people on the ladder might be too much total weight but he didn't want to show any fear in front of Marmaduke or Silas. Nor did he want to get left behind, not just for his own benefit but he didn't like the idea of Eloise being alone with the other two.

The ladder was long but every ten rungs it had been fastened securely to the cliff. The two chains were rusting in places but still looked strong enough. The bigger concern, particularly for Caleb going last, was the wooden rungs. Every now and then he heard a cracking from above and felt scraps of wood fall onto his head where one had broken. He suspected Marmaduke was deliberately stamping on them to make the going tougher for Caleb but he never managed to catch him in the act. It was taking all of his concentration to focus on his current position and the ladder above him was a challenge yet to be faced.

He swore quietly to himself when he came to three broken rungs in a row, forcing him to pull himself up using just his hands on the chains, but he didn't want to give Marmaduke the satisfaction of knowing it was causing him difficulty.

On and on they climbed. Caleb had never had a fear of heights on board the ship, often racing up to the giddy height of the crow's nest, but this was a whole new experience. Sweat was pouring off him, his hands becoming slippery and drips running from his forehead into his eyes making them sting. His soaked shirt was plastered to his skin. He paused to catch his breath and twisted round to look out to sea. The midday sun was high in the clear sky, turning the choppy water into a constantly flickering battle of blinding peaks. The Cutlass was still moored in its same position, a dark silhouette against the golden blue water, but The Unicorn was now a distant blur. Barrowclough and Yaro had moved the ship far out of range and were gliding slowly west, their sails mostly stowed as they relied on the mainsail alone.

A gentle breeze rocked the ladder and Caleb shivered slightly, aware that his damp shirt had cooled while he'd been staring out to sea. He needed to get moving or he'd be left behind. Keen to catch up he wiped his moist hands on his top and began climbing again, more quickly than before but still making sure he kept a firm grip on the sides in case there were any more breakages. He counted the rungs as he went and was well past a hundred when he finally dragged himself over the edge of the cliff top and onto safe ground.

Eloise was a short distance away studying the map

while the two pirates from The Cutlass spoke quietly nearby. Caleb rolled onto his back and breathed deeply. He felt strangely shaky after the climb, the tension from worrying about each rung of the ladder having built up in every muscle of his body. He had to force himself to stand and felt slightly dizzy as he looked briefly at the view before joining Eloise and the others.

'Look,' she said, pointing. 'The map has a picture of two trees on it, the left one underlined twice with two wavy lines. And over there, see? There are two palm trees which are larger than anything else around them.'

'You're bleeding,' grinned Silas as he put a handful of tobacco in his mouth and began chewing messily. 'That little climb too much for you was it?'

Caleb reached behind to feel his shirt. His hand came back covered in blood. Silas was right. The dampness wasn't just from sweat. He wiped his palm casually on the front of his shirt.

'It's just a scratch. Don't worry, I'll have no trouble keeping up with you.'

Marmaduke laughed then set off walking towards the tall palm tree. Silas spat a lump of tobacco at Caleb's feet then followed his captain. Caleb made to go after them but Eloise put a hand on his arm to stop him.

'You okay?'

Caleb nodded. 'I think so. It's sore but I'm used to it now. It looks worse than it feels.'

'Don't do anything strenuous if you can help it,' Eloise advised him. 'You don't want your wounds splitting open again.' She handed him a container of water and pulled out a couple of apples from her bag. 'Mind your step too,' she added, taking a bite. 'I think it's the other tree we need, not the left one. I have a feeling we're going to stumble on another of Marissa Cortez's traps very soon.'

Caleb looked at Marmaduke and Silas heading away from them and smiled. 'Let's hope so.'

25

As it was they reached the palm tree without any mishaps. Marmaduke and Silas were already resting in its shade sharing a flagon of rum when Eloise and Caleb entered the clearing. Caleb couldn't help wondering how anything survived on this barren island. The terrain was mostly sand and rock with just a few sparse shrubs and small trees somehow hanging onto life.

'You look disappointed Master Storm,' commented Marmaduke.

'Just hot,' Caleb replied, quickly trying to mask his face. Marmaduke was right, he was disappointed they hadn't encountered some nasty obstacle but he wasn't going to tell him that.

'Aye, that it is,' Marmaduke agreed, lifting his tricorne hat and wiping his brow. Caleb didn't know how he could stand it. He'd left his long blue coat on The Unicorn but the Duke was still dressed in his full captain's uniform.

'Where now then missy?' Marmaduke asked.

Eloise took out the scrap of map again. There wasn't much else recorded. 'Looks like we climb that rock over there,' she pointed. The ground sloped down gently away from them before rising steeply to a high point in the centre of the island. 'There's a cross on the map just before the peak. I guess we'll find something there.'

'Something?' asked Silas. 'The treasure?'

Eloise shrugged. 'I don't know. There are other crosses on the map. This is one of them, that's all.'

'We're getting close,' Silas said eagerly. 'I can feel it.'

'It could just be a pointer to the next clue,' warned Eloise.

Silas gave her an evil look. 'You'd better not be messing us about, ye cheating, gutless stowaway.'

Marmaduke chuckled nastily. 'Don't mind Silas, Miss Storm. He's just sore you got the better of him in Cooperstown. I'd watch what you say to him if I were you, he's itching to return the favour.' He reached out and ran his finger down Eloise's cheek.

Eloise flinched at Marmaduke's touch and glanced at Silas. He grinned as he twisted his knife in the air, deliberately reflecting sunlight into Eloise's eyes.

'He's itching because he's a foul-smelling, pox-ridden rat,' she replied, walking right up to him. From nowhere she produced her own knife, pushing it into his crotch. 'And if you come near me again it won't be your cheek I cut next time.'

Silas froze, but then just as swiftly conjured a second blade of his own, batting hers away as he slashed down with the other knife at Eloise's face.

She drew back quickly but Silas was fast and she felt the sting of his knife as it whooshed past. Ignoring the sharp pain she counter-attacked equally as rapidly, the two blades clanging together.

'Enough!' barked Marmaduke, grabbing Caleb's arm as he rushed to join in. The Duke's powerful command made Eloise and Silas jump apart, each one eyeing the other warily. 'You two can settle this another time. Right now we've more important things to do. Silas, sheath your blades and get moving.'

Silas smiled maliciously. 'Now we're even,' he said menacingly as he wiped his knife on his shirt and slid it into his belt. Eloise stood her ground, taking no notice of the blood she could feel trickling down her cheek.

'We need to watch him,' Caleb said quietly at her side as they watched Silas walk off in the direction of the peak. 'You okay? That looks nasty.'

'We need to watch both of them,' she replied as her gaze turned to Marmaduke, now walking impatiently only a couple of paces behind Silas. She wiped her face with her palm and looked at the blood on her hand. The cut was deeper than she'd realised and she knew she'd been fortunate not to lose an eye. 'So much for us going in pairs. Looks like those two are so eager to find the treasure first they've forgotten we're here.'

'We should hurry to catch up then,' Caleb told her.

'No,' Eloise insisted as she took out her carafe. She winced as she poured water over her cut. 'I'm sure there'll be a trap around here somewhere. I'm starting to get a feel for the way Marissa thinks. The crosses on the map, they're not for the treasure. They could be obstacles to watch out for, not to help us find it.'

'So where is the treasure then?'

Eloise shook her head. 'That I don't know. Marmaduke might be right about us needing both maps to find it. But until then let's let them find all the traps first shall we?'

Caleb grinned. 'I'm glad I'm on your side.'

They set off slowly, half watching the ground, half with an eye on the two pirates up ahead. There was always a chance they could get lucky and miss whatever obstacle was coming, leaving it for the twins to fall into instead. There was no obvious danger around them. Certainly nothing like the diverted waterfall or the sudden drop in the darkness of the tunnel. The whole area was as empty as it had been on the other side of the palm tree. Dry sand blew gently in the sea breeze and a few shrubs littered the landscape but otherwise there was nothing to see. Caleb figured they were probably near the very centre of the island now, at the furthest point from the sea in any direction. He could still see glimpses of shimmering blue but there was no sign of The Unicorn. He hoped the ship had been able to slip away from The Cutlass without any concerns.

'What's going on?' Eloise asked. Caleb had been staring out to sea but looked round to see Silas getting angry with Marmaduke about something. The two men had come to a stop and were arguing at the bottom of the steep climb up the rock. The twins crept nearer to see what the quarrel was about. It looked like they were fighting but in a very unusual manner. Marmaduke was in front, facing away from them, but had twisted around and grabbed hold of Silas with one hand. The first mate in turn was trying to push him off.

'They're stuck,' Caleb observed. They edged closer, just in time to see Silas pull out his knife and threaten Marmaduke. The captain snatched his arm away before Silas could attack him.

'It's quicksand,' Eloise breathed quietly as Silas fell and landed flat on his back in the boggy sludge. 'Don't get any closer.'

'Help me,' growled Marmaduke, both his feet refusing to move. He was deeper into the quicksand than Silas and was now up to his knees. The more he squirmed the deeper he appeared to sink.

'Keep still,' Eloise called out. 'You're making it worse.'

'I don't need advice from you lassie,' Marmaduke scowled. 'Just throw me a rope or something and pull me out.'

'We don't have a rope,' Caleb replied.

'Use your coat,' said Silas through gritted teeth. 'It's dragging you down anyway. Throw it to me and I'll pull you out.'

Marmaduke shrugged the coat off his shoulders and held onto one end as he tossed the rest towards Silas. The first mate grinned nastily and reached inside, pulling out the map of Claw Island.

'You double crossing thieving traitorous dog,' yelled Marmaduke. 'You'll pay for this.'

'Ignore him,' Silas called to the others. He was laying sprawled on the wet sand and was desperately trying to swim backwards towards the drier ground.

He was agonisingly close but the quicksand was sucking him forwards, the safety of the hard earth just out of reach. He realised his movements were causing the sticky sand to pull him further down and forced himself to relax. As he lay there, completely still, he stopped sinking and remained fixed on the surface. 'Get me out first then the three of us can rescue the captain.'

'Why would we want to do that?' Caleb called down, which earned him an angry look from Marmaduke. He was still fighting the sand but the struggle to move his feet was only causing him to sink lower. His legs were now fully submerged and the deeper he dropped the more stuck he became. 'I'm serious,' Caleb added. 'He'd let us drown in there without a second's thought.'

'Alright, forget the Duke, just throw me a rope,' Silas said calmly. He looked slightly foolish with his arms and legs spread wide in a star shape but he appeared to be safe for now, in stark contrast to his captain.

'Get me out!' snarled Marmaduke, panic growing on his face as he sank further up to his chest. He held his arms in the air desperately trying to keep them out of the wet sand.

'Keep still,' called Eloise. 'Any deeper and it'll take a dozen men to get you out of there. Stop moving and we can send your crew back later to get you.'

'There won't be a later if you don't help me,' spat Marmaduke. 'Try something. Anything!'

His long coat was laying on the surface behind Silas, way out of reach of Eloise and Caleb. She searched in her bag for any kind of rope or twine but there was nothing long enough to reach either man. Looking around she saw a long bough from an old tree, bleached white from years of lying under the bright sun. 'Don't move,' she told them. 'We're getting a branch to pull you out.'

'Me first,' Silas told her calmly. 'If you try to rescue the Duke from there he'll drag you in after him.'

'Why are we saving them?' Caleb whispered to Eloise when they got to the branch. 'Let them sink, I don't care.'

'Silas can rot for all I care but he has the other map,' she reminded him quietly. 'We may still need it. Now help me with this.'

Between them they carried the branch back to the quicksand. Silas was where they'd left him but Marmaduke, fighting it with all his strength, was now in real danger as the sand touched his neck. He twisted left and right, lifting his chin as far as he could, his hands still raised high.

'Lose your weapons first,' Eloise ordered. 'Sword and knives. Drop them in the sand or we leave you where you are.'

Silas carefully unbuckled his sword then slowly lifted his long knife in the air and flung it out of reach. It plopped onto the surface where it lay stuck for a moment before it sank and disappeared from sight.

'Alright, hold on,' said Eloise as she and Caleb dropped the branch, partly on solid ground with the bulk of it resting on top of the sticky sand. They both sat on their end to keep it in place as Silas slowly reached for it and tried pulling himself along on his back. The thick branch slid towards him and the twins both dug their heels into the earth to hold it in place.

Bit by bit Silas inched closer to safety, breathing heavily with the effort but remaining calm. Finally his hand touched the solid floor and he twisted onto his stomach to haul himself out.

'Now you can get the Duke,' gasped Silas as he lay there panting.

'Too late,' Eloise replied as she looked up to see the sand close in around Marmaduke's face. He took a few panicked breaths then his head disappeared leaving only his hat and arms sticking out of the sand. They pushed the branch towards his flailing hands but it wasn't quite long enough to reach him. Eloise and Caleb watched in horror as Marmaduke waved his arms hopelessly looking for something to grab onto before they too sank out of sight, the long coat and his three-sided hat all that remained. A few bubbles appeared on the surface for a moment before popping, then everything went quiet. The captain was gone.

26

'You don't seem too upset,' Eloise said as the three of them backed away from the quicksand. Silas had insisted they make no effort to recover Marmaduke and had been keen to depart the area as soon as possible.

'I've seen a lot of men die,' Silas replied. 'Goes with the trade. We'll raise a cup of rum to him later then that'll be it.'

They cautiously skirted the edge of the basin and safely made it round to the base of the rock on the far side. Caleb couldn't help checking back regularly for any movement but all was still, the long white branch lying undisturbed on the surface. The twins began scrambling up the steep slope first, Silas content to stay behind and let them find the safe route.

'Well, on the downside Marmaduke is dead,' Caleb said solemnly as he clambered higher. The rock face was smooth and baked warm by the sun as he pulled himself up. 'But on the plus side,' he added happily. 'Marmaduke is dead!'

Eloise rolled her eyes as they continued climbing. The cut on her cheek had stopped bleeding although the left side of her face was now matted with blood and she could feel it throbbing. She forced it from her mind as she scrambled up the rocky crag. It was almost vertical in places but not particularly high and they were soon at the point where the cross was marked on the map.

'There's nothing here,' Silas said angrily when he joined them. They searched the area for ten minutes but it was empty with no markings anywhere. The only feature in sight was the circle of quicksand far below them.

'This doesn't make sense,' Eloise said, looking at the map again. She looked back at the palm tree then at where they were standing. They were precisely where the X on the map was marked.

'Well we can't dig,' Caleb pointed out, stamping on the ground a couple of times. 'This is solid rock.'

'Give me the other map,' Eloise said to Silas suddenly. He looked at her for a moment then slowly reached inside his jacket and pulled it out, reluctantly handing it over. Eloise held the two maps side by side, her eyes flicking between the drawings of the two islands. As well as the other symbols both had X markings drawn over them, some large, others smaller. 'These can't be for the treasure,' she told them. 'Look, this one's in the sea.'

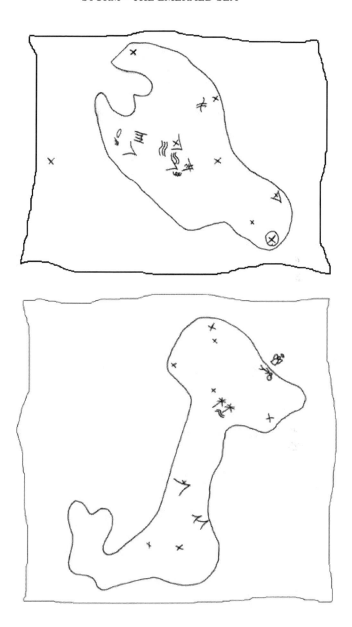

'A rock offshore maybe?' asked Caleb, gazing out towards the horizon.

Eloise turned the maps onto their sides to view them from a different angle but it made no difference to the outcome. Then she noticed something. 'Wait a minute,' she murmured to herself. Placing one map on top of the other she lined up the bottom of the J with the heart shaped bay. The hook slotted perfectly in the outline of the water so that the rest of the J wrapped itself around Claw Island.

'They go together,' marvelled Silas, watching her closely.

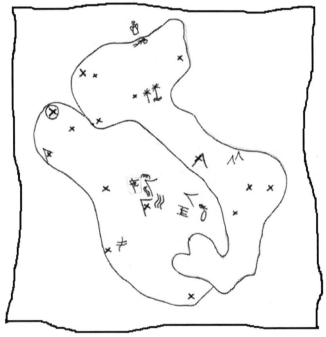

Eloise held the two maps up in the air to get a clearer image. With the sunlight shining through they blended into a single picture. It only took Silas a moment to spot it.

'That X was in the sea on the first map. It's now here on this island. On land.'

Caleb looked more closely at the cross on the map then to the east. The sun was reflecting brightly off the sea in the distance and he had to shield his eyes but he could make out a small copse of trees roughly where the map suggested.

Without warning he suddenly felt a huge thump in his stomach. He gasped as he was winded, the air blown out of him. As he struggled for breath he felt himself being pushed backwards. Too late he realised he was standing on the very edge of the rock. Silas was forcing him towards the drop but he was too dazed to fight it. With a sickening feeling he felt the ground disappear beneath his feet then he was falling, rolling head over heels, plummeting down the slope.

'No!' shouted Eloise, drawing her sword as she chased after Silas.

'You don't want to be wasting time with that,' mocked Silas as he dodged to one side to avoid her thrust. 'Looks like your brother landed in the quicksand. If you want to save him you'd better get down there.'

Eloise hesitated but knew Silas was right. She made sure to keep a safe distance from the pirate as she ran to the edge and started lowering herself. The last glimpse she had of Silas he was hurrying off to the east towards the treasure.

Looking down as she went Eloise could see Caleb sprawled in the sand. He began moving and a wave of relief swept over her as she realised he was still alive. The feeling was instantly replaced by dread as she saw him sink quickly into the sand.

'Stop struggling!' she called down, but Caleb didn't seem to hear her. He suddenly seemed to understand where he was and began frantically trying to swim to the side of the wet bog but it only made matters worse. Eloise hurried on, sending little stones tumbling ahead of her as she slid down the rock. She was wary of falling into the sand herself but desperate to reach Caleb before he disappeared from view.

She slid down the last slab of rock and turned to see Caleb almost completely submerged. The suction from the sand was dragging him further down every time he moved so that only his neck and head were above the surface.

'Keep still!' shouted Eloise. Caleb saw her and stopped thrashing about.

'Can you get the branch?' he called. Eloise nodded and ran around the edge of the bowl to where they'd been standing before. The branch was still lying on top of the quicksand with only a small portion of one end resting safely on the firmer ground. When she tried lifting it the whole thing remained stubbornly glued to the sticky sand, barely moving at all despite her efforts. She changed position and dug her feet in trying to drag it towards her instead. It shifted slightly but as she paused to take a breath the sand sucked it straight back to its previous position.

'It won't budge,' called Eloise. 'Wait there, I'll try to find another one.'

'Wait here,' muttered Caleb, lifting his chin to

keep his mouth clear of the sand. 'Take your time, I'm not going anywhere.'

There were no branches large enough nearby so Eloise ran further away searching for anything which would be able to reach Caleb. There was nothing other than a few brittle looking twigs that would snap the second she tried to use them.

'It's hopeless,' Eloise shouted as she ran back to the quicksand. 'The place is empty. Can you hang on long enough for me to fetch Barrowclough and Yaro?'

'No chance,' Caleb gasped, spitting sand from his mouth. 'I have an idea. Come as close as you safely can. Careful not to step in this stuff though. I mean it, don't risk yourself as well. I'm taking off my belt. I'll try to throw one end to you.'

Eloise ran round to the closest point to Caleb. A rock was sitting on the edge of the quicksand and she pushed her foot against it to test its stability. It stayed securely where it was so she kept one foot braced on that while she leaned forwards to wait for the belt. Caleb had to move as slowly as possible, gently pushing his hands into the thick, gloopy sand until they reached his waist. Ever so carefully he unknotted the belt and gradually pulled it through the loops, making sure to hold on as tightly as he could. If he dropped it now there would be no chance.

He felt the end come free and little by little slowly raised his hands. His confidence grew as they moved higher through the sludge and he picked up speed in his excitement. The quicksand suddenly made a low gurgling sound and he felt himself sink a tiny fraction, causing him to let out a small yelp. He had to look straight up to the sky to keep his face clear of the sand but finally after what felt like an age his hands eventually broke the surface.

'We'll only have one shot at this,' Caleb called out. 'When I throw it I'm going to get pulled under. If it's too far out of reach don't try to get it, okay? There's no point both of us dying.'

'I'm not letting you die,' Eloise shouted. Caleb's ears were below the sand so she wasn't sure he could hear her.

'Forget Silas,' Caleb said. 'Get back to the ship and take the girl home. Now get ready to catch.'

'Wait!' yelled Eloise. Caleb paused and stretched his neck as far as he could to hear her better. 'Put the tube in your mouth,' continued Eloise, shouting as loudly as she could. 'Remember Tarian said it's hollow. Use it to breathe through until I can get you out.'

'Eloise, you're a genius!' Caleb shouted, a big grin spreading across his face. He felt for the end of the belt. 'Okay, here goes,' he called. He took a deep breath and put it in his mouth then hurled the rest as far as he could towards Eloise's voice. The quicksand immediately engulfed him, the sloppy wet slush oozing over his face and sending him into darkness.

He couldn't tell if his throw had been successful or not and held his breath for as long as he could. It was an eerie feeling floating in the quicksand. The floor beneath him wasn't solid and he could slowly move his legs against the pressure all around him. It felt like he was floating and if he hadn't just left the surface he wasn't sure he'd know which way was up. He tried making a walking motion as if he was on solid ground but couldn't tell if it was making any difference.

His eyes were closed against the gritty wetness and he kept one hand clamped tightly on the thin hose. When he couldn't hold his breath any longer he blew a little of it out then sucked on the tube. A thin trickle of air crept into his lungs. It was painfully uncomfortable but might just be enough to keep him alive a little longer.

Meanwhile Eloise was above looking at the other end of Caleb's belt. His throw had been excellent, directly towards her, but it had fallen short. A whole body length short. There was no way she could grab hold of it from where she was standing. The rope lay there, just out of reach. She almost felt as though it was laughing at her. She was so close to being able to do something, so near and yet so far.

Caleb was right about one thing. She couldn't afford to fall in as well or she'd never be able to rescue him. She tested the ground around her until she was confident she knew where the edge was then took out her curved sword and lay down. Her whole body was safely on the solid earth but her head and arms now floated above the quicksand. She turned the sword so that she was holding the blade between her palms and stretched forwards. The hilt hovered precariously above the clasp of Caleb's belt. She was going to have to be careful not to mess this up and push the belt under again. She took a deep breath, concentrating everything on the hilt of the sword, then lowered it.

'Yes!' she said to herself as it hooked the metal clasp. Gently, Eloise pulled the belt towards her, nervously watching it slide over the wet sand. The weight of the weapon was making her arms shake and she noticed both the sword and the belt beginning to sink lower. She kept pulling, gripping the sharp blade with one hand as she bent her elbow back. 'No!' she cried as the belt came loose and disappeared below the surface.

27

Beneath the quicksand Caleb tried to take a deep breath but this time no air came. The other end of the hollow tube must have got blocked. He tried to blow out to clear it but didn't have enough air left in his lungs. Panic started to overwhelm him as he realised that might already have been his last breath.

Eloise threw her sword behind her and plunged her arm into the sand. It was thick and heavy, pushing against her as she felt around in slow motion for the belt. Her fingers reached out, searching left and right. There! She brushed against it and grabbed hold, dragging it up into the air. Anxiously she pulled and pulled until the belt went taut then stood and tied it around her own waist. Leaning backwards she saw more of it gradually start to emerge from the sand.

In the darkness Caleb sensed the belt pull away from him. Sucking with all his might he felt a massive relief as air filled his lungs again. He held on tightly to the belt with both hands and continued his painstaking walking motion but now he had the feeling there was a purpose to it. He knew which direction he was travelling even if it was slow going. He nearly stumbled as his foot unexpectedly hit solid floor. He was still completely submerged in the quicksand but the ground beneath him was sloping upwards.

Eloise braced her legs against the rock on the edge of the sand and pulled with all her strength. She was leaning at a steep angle wondering if they were ever going to make it when she suddenly saw Caleb's hair appear on the surface. The sight of him gave her a renewed energy and she gave the belt another huge heave, laughing deliriously as the rest of his head followed. He wiped wet sand from his eyes and let out a loud whooping cheer. Gradually more and more of him emerged until he finally collapsed safely next to Eloise.

He took several deep lungfuls of air, gazing up at the sun happily. 'Let's not do that again,' he finally managed to gasp. He took a long swig of water and wiped his mouth, then poured more from the flagon over his head to wash off the worst of the sand. 'So now we go after Silas,' Caleb added when he'd recovered enough to stand up.

'I don't think that's a good idea,' Eloise replied, a glint in her eye. 'He went the wrong way.'

Caleb raised an eyebrow at her. 'What aren't you telling me?'

'Look at the crosses again,' Eloise told him, handing over both maps. Caleb lined them up, one on top of the other so that Hook Island and Claw Island were neatly entwined, then held them up to the sky to get a clearer picture of the two combined.

'Okay, so we know it's the Gemini constellation,' Caleb said. 'Castor here, Pollux there.' He gasped. 'But Alhena is missing. There should be another X somewhere around ... here.' He put his finger on the map at the far southwest tip of the island. 'So this is a treasure map,' he said quietly. 'With everything marked except the location of the treasure.'

'X doesn't mark the spot,' Eloise said with a grin.

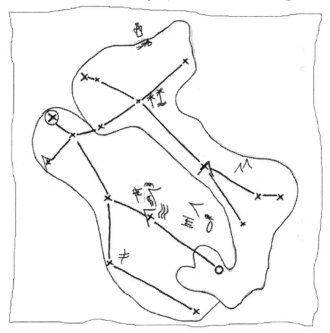

They decided to climb the rock again for a better view but the second they reached the top they could see immediately where to aim for. The southern area of the island far greener than the north but hidden among the trees they knew without a doubt where they needed to head. The missing star would have been placed exactly over a crater that was just visible from their high position.

'You'd walk right past it if you didn't know it was there,' marvelled Eloise. 'We'll need to be careful to make sure we don't lose it.'

Caleb glanced up at the sun. It had already moved way past the highest point and was now edging further west. 'We'd better get a move on too,' he pointed out. 'Barrowclough can only keep the ship in the bay at high tide remember.'

They hurried down the slope, losing sight of the crater immediately but aiming for a particular tree that wasn't far from their target. The land was initially dry and dusty like the rest of the north side of the island but the further they went the more vegetation appeared around them. Soon they were pushing through thick undergrowth and Caleb had to take out his sword to hack a clear path.

He was sweating heavily when they broke out into a rocky clearing and saw the opening of the crater in front of them. It was no bigger than the width of the ship, with jagged rocky edges all around it.

'I really hope the treasure isn't down there,' Eloise said, leaning over to peer inside. Far below deep blue water swirled back and forth, crashing white frothy spray up the sides of the crater.

'Are you sure we have the right place?' Caleb asked, trepidation clear in his voice. 'We'll be smashed to pieces if we fall in that.'

'It has to be here,' Eloise insisted. 'Or near here somewhere. See if you can find anything interesting.'

They made their way carefully around the circumference of the crater, Eloise checking out the trees and bushes by the edge of the clearing while Caleb stayed closer to the mouth of the hole. 'Look,' he called over. 'There, about halfway down. Does that look like a gap to you?'

Eloise ran to join him and they strained their eyes at the rock face opposite. It was above the water line where the waves smacked loudly against the sides, but they could both see the dampness of the walls reaching higher.

'Looks like it's underwater at high tide,' Eloise observed. 'But you're right, it's some kind of opening. I guess we're going down there after all.'

They'd learned their lesson from the tunnel on Claw Island so quickly went to work collecting the branches and tree resin needed to make torches. Once ready they made their way to the far side until they were standing directly over the narrow hole. There was fortunately no need for ropes, the rough edges of the crater walls posing no difficulties for either of the twins to climb down, although the booming noise of the sea echoed around them more and more loudly as they descended making the journey far more nerve-wracking than it would have been normally.

Eloise got to the opening first and stepped gratefully into the dark, damp channel. She already had one of the torches lit when Caleb appeared behind her. They had to walk in single file, the passage only wide enough for them to go one at a time.

'Do you get the feeling we're going to stumble into

another of Marissa's nasty surprises,' Caleb said from behind Eloise.

'I'll almost be disappointed if we don't,' Eloise replied.

'One thing I don't understand,' Caleb said as they advanced cautiously down the tunnel. 'Wade gave us the map for Claw Island but why didn't he just tell us to come straight here?'

'I think he wanted us to earn it,' Eloise replied. 'The treasure has been hidden for fifty years. He couldn't let just anyone find it. Remember he asked us if we knew our stars? He needed to know we had the knowledge to follow the clues without making it easy for us.'

'Or without Marmaduke being able to torture the location out of us,' Caleb added. 'The less we knew, the better.'

'Exactly,' Eloise agreed, then chuckled. 'I wonder how Silas is getting on searching the other side of the island?'

'I hope he's fallen into another one of Marissa's traps,' scowled Caleb, rubbing his stomach as he remembered the punch that had left him helpless before Silas had thrown him into the quicksand.

'Shh,' Eloise said abruptly. 'Can you hear that?'

Caleb nodded. 'Water. Up ahead. Watch your step.'

The passageway grew steadily wider as they crept forwards, the sound of falling water getting louder with every step. The flickering light from the torch flame suddenly lit up the right hand wall, the firelight reflecting mesmerisingly off a smooth sheet of water cascading beside them.

'Pretty,' commented Eloise as the light danced across the shimmering water.

'Should we be nervous?' asked Caleb. 'This has to be here for a reason, don't you think?'

'Look,' said Eloise pointing at the top of the wall of water. A long horizontal slit had been chiselled into the top of the rock wall where the water was now flowing through. 'This is man-made.'

'Strange,' Caleb said thoughtfully. 'There must be a reservoir or underground lake behind here. Probably gets refilled at every high tide.' He reached up and ran his fingers across the bottom of the thin opening. The water splayed out on both sides of his hand and opened up a brief gap in the otherwise solid sheet of water.

'Do that again,' Eloise said, leaning in more closely with the torch. Caleb put his palm back to part the water and stood aside so that his sister could look through the gap more easily.

'There's another tunnel,' she gasped. She looked to her left to see the passage they were standing in disappear into the darkness ahead. 'It's not a trap,' she said to Caleb. 'It's a door.'

She held her forearm against the flow of water to widen the gap then quickly thrust the flaming torch through the opening. Ducking her head into the space she could see the wet floor looked solid so without a word stepped forwards. The water dropped back down behind her, instantly hiding her from Caleb. The tunnel he was still in was plunged into darkness but he could easily see the dancing orange flame beyond the sheet of water in front of him. Parting it again he jumped through to join her.

A narrow fissure led off to their left. After only a short distance they came to some steps which had been roughly chiselled into the rock. The bottom four were green and slimy, years of daily tides taking their toll, but after that the rest were clean and dry. Eloise led the way, placing her feet extra carefully until she was past the slippery section. They had to crouch at the top to get through an opening into a large room that extended into the darkness.

Neither of them moved. Caleb could tell his mouth was open but no sound came out. For once in his life he was utterly speechless. They were standing in a wide, low cavern, and stretching out before them filling the entire space were thousands and thousands of twinkling blue and green gems.

28

It was immediately obvious there were far too many jewels for them to carry. Caleb had spent a long time laughing and laying among the glittering stones, picking them up and letting them fall through his fingers. Eloise had been more cautious, studying a handful of them closely in the firelight.

'We'll have to leave them here of course,' she'd told him when he'd calmed down for a moment. 'There are way too many for us to carry and it wouldn't be safe to have them all on one ship anyway.'

Caleb nodded. 'We can take some though, right? Fill your bag and my pockets?'

'Of course,' Eloise replied. 'But we'll need to be careful. We can't just walk into the first port we come to with a bagful of riches. Every pirate in the Caribbean will be after us.'

'Including Silas,' Caleb said. 'Good. Let him come. We'll hire men to string him up and drag him under our ship, see how he likes it.'

'We don't have men yet,' pointed out Eloise. 'And he's still on this island somewhere. He'll never find this place without the maps but the crew of The Cutlass outnumber us twenty to one. If we don't get away before sunset we'll be in real danger.'

That thought spurred them both to get moving but after collecting as many gems as they could carry they soon realised Silas wasn't their only threat. As they reluctantly left the cavern, taking one last longing look at the hypnotic floor of jewels, they descended the steps to discover the passage was already sloshing with sea water.

'The tide,' said Caleb, stepping into it nervously. 'It's rising. We need to move, now.'

They hurried through the curtain of water hiding the entrance to the secret room. The flow was slower than when they'd first discovered it but they both knew the incoming tide would refill the reservoir feeding it and the sheet of water would be back to full strength soon. Until then they still had to make their way to the entrance, a journey which was now hampered by the sea washing in almost up to their knees.

They found their way back to the opening in the crater but the sight was a world away from their arrival only an hour before. If they hadn't both spent years at sea the thundering sound of the foaming surf crashing all around them in the enclosed space would have been terrifying. As it was Caleb still felt his heart pounding as they climbed away from the tumultuous waters. If they'd waited any longer they would have been trapped inside the cavern until the tide subsided and by then it would have been too late to reach the Unicorn.

As it was they realised they'd already spent too long searching for the treasure and had to run to get to the beach on the west coast. The sun was edging ever lower as they broke through the trees. They were now standing on the cliff top in the northern side of the J's hook at the bottom end of the island. Off to their right Caleb could see the rocky peak he'd been thrown off and way in the distance were the two tall palm trees closer to the top of the island.

Directly in front of them was the churning, boiling sea. Several jagged rocks jutted out from the water, white spray thrown high in the air as chaotic waves collided with them. The falling sun was already turning the sky into beautiful shades of pink and copper which reflected brilliantly off the water.

But it was a water with no sign of any ship. Caleb scanned the horizon but there wasn't a vessel in sight.

'Where's The Unicorn?' he asked with concern. 'She should be here by now.'

'Maybe Barrowclough had to wait,' said Eloise. 'The tide's only just coming in. He wouldn't have been able to get close yet. Let's head to the beach.'

The ground sloped away to their right so they hurried along the cliff edge looking for a path to the sand. When they were halfway down Eloise suddenly called out.

'Look! The ship!' She pointed to where the Unicorn was just appearing from behind the southwest headland. The long, twisted horn pointing out of the prow was glittering in the late sun as it rose and fell on the waves. Caleb smiled and waved although he couldn't tell if anyone on board had seen them. The sight of the boat was enough to give them a renewed energy as they continued to run down to the water's edge.

The Unicorn was light, sitting high in the water, but was still too sizeable a ship to come right in to the beach. It dropped anchor offshore then a few moments later the tender was untied from behind and began making its way towards them. The waves rolled relentlessly under it, picking it up and dropping it down again every few seconds. Caleb began to wonder whether this was such a good idea; the trip back out to the ship was going to be hard going.

'Is that Barrowclough or Yaro?' Eloise asked, watching the back of the sailor as they drew closer. The sun was directly behind the larger ship now. The small tender was a dark shadow in comparison.

'Can't tell,' Caleb replied. 'But I hope he gets a move on or it'll be dark by the time we get out there.'

A big wave suddenly caught the tiny boat and it shot forwards, riding on the crest for several seconds before falling back into the trough. The next wave wasn't far behind, picking it up again where this time the little tender was able to surf all the way to the beach. It was only as it was scraping onto the sand that the twins realised everything had gone horribly wrong. Jasper was alone in the boat and turned to look at Caleb apologetically.

'How? What are you doing here?' Caleb spluttered.

'Sorry mate,' Jasper replied, jumping over the side and holding on to the bucking craft still being pushed and pulled by the waves. 'I've been sent to get you.'

'By whom?' Eloise asked, dreading the answer.

'Silas,' Jasper answered sadly. Caleb was his friend and he knew what this meant. 'We had orders to take your ship once you were out of sight on the island. The Cutlass went west, our tender went east to cover both coasts. Barrowclough evaded us of course, he's way better than anyone we had on board. But when he came back to pick you up we were waiting. They didn't stand a chance.'

Caleb glanced out to sea to look at The Unicorn. As he did, The Cutlass appeared from behind the headland, floating menacingly offshore in the deeper water. It looked huge compared to their ship, the black hull with its three masts towering over the small sloop. Even the large black and scarlet Jolly Roger flapping malevolently in the breeze was enough to strike fear into Caleb. He'd always been on board in the past and for the first time had a taste of what other sailors must have felt as The Cutlass bore down on them.

'But – Silas?' Caleb stammered.

'Don't know much about that,' Jasper replied. 'He appeared about an hour ago on our tender. They must have picked him up on the east coast then come round to find us. He didn't have the captain with him, I guess he's still on the island somewhere. We already had The Unicorn by then. And now he's sent me to bring you two back.'

Caleb shook his head. 'Not a chance. I'd rather die here than give him the satisfaction of killing me.'

'He said you'd say that,' Jasper said miserably. 'He also said to tell you that he has the girl and that she's going to die a very slow and painful death unless you hand over the treasure.'

29

Even with the three of them it was hard work rowing out through the waves. The high tide meant some of the rocks offshore had become submerged just below the surface and twice they felt a worrying scrape on the bottom of their boat as they ploughed on.

The Unicorn was closest, its lighter hull sitting much higher in the water than the vast pirate ship. Caleb, facing the shore as he rowed, watched the island recede. He was angry and frustrated that a short time before he and Eloise had become the richest people in the Caribbean and now they were helpless at the mercy of a ruthless pirate.

Long shadows formed on the land as the sun touched the horizon and the cliff face faded from a bright pink to a more spooky light grey. The choppy sea darkened and quickly turned into an unwelcoming sight, a far cry from the beautiful and inviting turquoise it had been only a short time before. Despite his growing dread at what was to come Caleb almost felt a sense of relief as they reached the Unicorn. A rope ladder was thrown down to them and Jasper gestured for the twins to climb up while he secured the boat.

'You're a hard boy to kill, Storm,' greeted Silas as Caleb heaved himself over the rail. The pirate was sitting on a crate and gently spinning the hilt of a sword between his thumb and forefinger as its tip cut a small notch into the deck.

'Aar! Storm! Storm!' called Archimedes from inside his cage. Silas glanced at it amused then returned his attention to Caleb as Eloise appeared behind and climbed onboard the ship.

'The treasure wasn't where the map said,' Silas said casually. 'But of course you know that don't you?' He stopped spinning his sword and looked at the twins carefully. Neither said a word. Caleb tried to look relaxed as he cast his gaze over the ship. Barrowclough and Yaro had been tied back to back against the mast. Ramsay, one of the gunners on The Cutlass, was holding his arm around Celeste's neck, a long knife in his other hand. Douglas, Talbot and Finlay were all standing nearby. After Silas, Caleb knew they were four of the cruellest pirates he'd ever sailed with, each one taking a sadistic pleasure in killing the unfortunate crews who crossed their paths.

'Let the girl go,' Caleb replied, bringing his attention back to Silas.

'Let the girl go, captain,' Silas mimicked. 'I'm in charge now. You found the treasure?'

'Maybe we did, maybe we didn't,' Caleb replied.

He had to seize onto the rail edging the ship to keep his balance in the rough sea. 'Let her go. Captain,' he added with disgust.

'Tell you what. How about you answer my question and I won't kill her.'

'No,' Eloise replied. 'We didn't find the treasure.'

'In that case I don't need the girl. Ramsay, throw her overboard.'

The pirate restraining Celeste grinned and pushed her towards the edge of the ship. They staggered left and right crossing the deck as the vessel was thrown around in the foreboding sea. Celeste squirmed and writhed as she struggled to break free but the pirate was too experienced to make any mistake. He reached the rail and lifted Celeste easily, ready to throw her over.

'Wait!' shouted Eloise and Caleb at the same time. They were a fair distance from shore and the jagged rocks hidden just below the churning waves would have torn her to shreds long before Celeste made it. Caleb wasn't even sure if she could swim. Ramsay paused and held the small girl in the air, his feet widely spaced to help him keep his balance as the ship rolled about in the tumultuous sea.

'Show me,' growled Silas.

Slowly, Eloise unfastened her bag and lifted out a clear green emerald the size of her thumb. Silas sat up straighter as she held it aloft, licking his lips with anticipation of what else might be in Eloise's bag.

'We found the treasure,' Eloise confirmed, throwing the jewel to Silas to inspect. She took a few steps to her right while he was distracted. 'Now let the girl go and we'll talk.'

Silas caught the gem and stared at it hungrily for a few seconds then nodded to Ramsay, who looked disappointed as he lowered Celeste to the floor and pushed her away. She ran to Caleb and hugged him tightly. 'It's okay,' he whispered. 'We won't let them hurt you.'

Eloise reached again into her bag causing Silas to look over excitedly. Instead she took out her brush and began to pull it roughly through her knotted hair. 'The sea air,' she explained as she stepped further away from the edge of the ship. 'Plays havoc with it.'

'I'm curious,' Silas said, his gaze returning to the emerald. He turned it over and over in his hand as he inspected it. 'There were no other crosses on the map. How did you find it?'

'I'll tell you,' Eloise replied. She stopped next to the mast where Barrowclough and Yaro were tied up. 'After you're back on The Cutlass and I know we're safe.'

Silas grunted. 'And give you a chance to set sail without revealing the secret? No chance.'

Caleb glanced around the ship. Ramsay was still standing by the rail to his left. Then came Silas sitting on the crate. Eloise was in the middle, next to their two captive crewmates. Then finally the three other pirates with many years of savage battles between them, all grouped together by the foredeck. It was five against two and all five were fearsome fighters. Silas knew that, and Caleb knew the new captain of The Cutlass could be confident that if he gave the order his men would very quickly overpower the twins.

But Caleb could also see what Eloise was planning.

He quietly pushed Celeste behind him and casually rested his hand on the hilt of his sword.

'Aar! No chance! No chance!' squawked Archimedes. Silas chuckled and stood up, walking over to look at the parrot. He slapped the cage with the side of his sword, laughing as the parrot fell and flapped around inside.

'I was going to eat you,' he said, opening the door of the cage and grabbing Archimedes. 'Aar, no chance, you said it,' he mocked as he pulled it out. 'Listen to the bird lass. He's smarter than you.' Silas lifted his free hand to stroke the parrot. In a flash it ducked its head and clamped its beak onto his outstretched finger.

Silas yelped and Eloise seized her chance. While the rest of the crew sniggered at their new captain she pulled the knife from her hairbrush and sawed through the rope tying the two men to the mast. Caleb took his opportunity too, lunging forwards and thrusting both his palms onto the surprised Ramsay's chest. The pirate had no time to react as he fell against the rail and toppled over the side. Climbing back on board would be difficult in the rough sea so Caleb knew he was now safely out of the way. One down, four to go. Drawing his sword he turned to face Silas.

30

The three pirates at the other end of the deck moved quickly. Douglas was closest and swung his giant sabre at Eloise as she cut through the final strands of rope. She dropped to the floor and rolled away just as the blade flashed past, missing her head by a whisker as it slammed into the mast.

Barrowclough and Yaro were still tied by one hand but were now free of the mast and they spun round to defend themselves against the two pirates racing towards them. Talbot had leapt forwards to attack but after years spent obeying Barrowclough's commands the sight of his former quartermaster caused him to hesitate for a moment. Seizing their chance the two captives ran straight at him. The rope joining their wrists caught him round the neck and threw him to the floor where his sword skittered away.

Yaro was fastest, picking it up just in time to deflect an almighty swing from Finlay's axe, but he hadn't had time to grip the sword fully and as the two weapons clanged together it flew from his hand. Finlay's heavy two headed blade was a fearsome sight and had been known to slice through an opponent's limbs during battle. He was always one of the first men to board an enemy ship, the grizzled pirate terrifying his victims as he cleared a path for others to follow. Right now he had a mad look in his eyes as he yelled out a war cry and heaved his axe back for another strike.

Yaro didn't hesitate and threw himself onto Finlay before he could swing his heavy weapon round for another blow. Barrowclough, who'd been about to land a huge thump on Talbot was yanked backwards. Off balance as the ship rocked up and down he stumbled and fell into Yaro and Finlay sending all three men crashing into an oil lamp which smashed against the smaller of the two masts. Flames instantly leapt at its base casting the ship in a flickering orange glow.

Eloise had already sprung to her feet, the knife still in one hand as she unsheathed her curved sword with the other. Douglas bared his crooked teeth and advanced, stabbing forwards with his longer sabre. The blade pierced her bag but stopped short of cutting into her body. As he pulled it back it ripped open a tear and emeralds spilled onto the deck, sliding away as the ship rolled in the waves. Several skidded to the rails lining the edge of the boat and disappeared over the side.

Distracted by the glittering jewels, Douglas suddenly found himself on the receiving end of a barrage of blows from Eloise, her sword a blur as she attacked in a fury. One side of her face was covered in dry blood from the wound inflicted by Silas, making her appear even more intimidating in the light from the fire. Douglas parried desperately but then Eloise slipped on a jewel and left herself open. Douglas grinned, lifting his sabre ready to unleash an assault of his own. Too late he realised Eloise had fooled him. With her sword held out wide in an apparent loss of balance he'd failed to notice the knife in her other hand. Driving it upwards the blade pierced his shirt and sank deep into his belly.

Silas's sword was in his hand before Caleb had taken a step. He threw the parrot to one side and lifted it in a mock salute. 'Let's see if you've been paying attention then, boy.'

Caleb knew he wouldn't be able to fight Silas and protect Celeste at the same time. He sidestepped two paces to his left then circled back again, holding the young girl behind him the whole time. Silas matched his every move, prowling menacingly in front of him, his guard up. Caleb wasn't looking for an opening though. He took another step to his right, his eyes locked on Silas's.

'Up the rigging, Celeste,' he ordered, his sword ready to parry any attack. Celeste understood and moved quickly, climbing onto the rail running along the edge of the ship and scampering up the rope ladder to safety.

'Just you and me now, boy,' Silas grinned nastily. He whipped his sword down to Caleb's left. Caleb blocked it but Silas was already swinging it round in a big loop aimed at Caleb's hip. Again, he blocked. They parted for a moment, stalking each other carefully as the boat rose and fell beneath their feet.

'Tell me Storm,' said Silas as he aimed another blow which Caleb managed to block. 'Is this treasure worth dying for?'

Caleb struck his own attack, a glancing blow which Silas easily parried. 'It's worth it,' Caleb answered. 'Just to stop you getting your filthy hands on it. You'll never find it, you know.'

'Maybe,' Silas acknowledged. 'Maybe not.' He stepped to his right two paces then ducked swiftly back to his left and aimed another shot. Caleb had nearly been fooled by the change in direction but was quick enough to react and block the pirate's sword. He knew Silas was trying to distract him by talking, goading him into thinking more about what he was saying rather than concentrating on the contest. But Caleb was under no illusions. This was a fight to the death and it would take all of his skill and concentration to survive.

'I know the treasure must be in the south of the island,' Silas continued, constantly moving as he looked for a better attacking position. 'You didn't have time to go north then back to the beach in time. And you didn't follow me to the east. So it's in the southwest. And let's face it, this isn't the biggest island in the Caribbean. What do you think it'll take me? One week? Two? I'll find it boy, you can be sure of that. I can smell bounty from ten leagues away. That treasure will be mine.'

'Not if I can help it,' Caleb said, and attacked ferociously, his sword moving faster than he'd ever fought before. Left and right, high and low, Caleb's blade beat down on Silas relentlessly and it was the pirate's turn to give his full attention to resisting the onslaught.

Behind, unnoticed by either of them Douglas dropped to his knees in shock. His sabre fell to the floor and he held his hands to his stomach. The knife was buried up to the hilt and he tried to pull it out but the blade was stuck fast. His face went pale and blood appeared at the corners of his mouth as he fell to one side. Eloise turned to see Talbot scrambling to stand and rejoin the attack. Barrowclough and Yaro were tangled with Finlay and the rolling ship was making it difficult for anyone to get to their feet. Only Finlay still had his weapon but it was impossible for him to swing his axe from his position and the fight had been reduced to an untidy brawl. Punches and kicks were being thrown wildly. Barrowclough took an elbow to the stomach as Yaro landed a fist on Finlay's chin, splitting his lip.

Talbot saw his own sword on the deck and dove on it. Eloise wanted to go to Caleb. The two of them together could beat Silas and put an end to the whole fight but Talbot was rising with his sword in his hand, his eyes on the unarmed Yaro and Barrowclough. Her crewmates would be cut down in seconds. A quick glance in Caleb's direction told her he was holding his own. She skipped over Douglas and, just as Talbot swung his sword down at Yaro's bare back she thrust out her own blade flat against Yaro's skin.

Talbot's blade clattered into Eloise's and slid harmlessly off to the side. Yaro might have earned a long bruise but no worse than that. Talbot was angry at being thwarted and snapped the back of his hand up, smashing it into Eloise's face and sending her sprawling across the deck. A stab of pain shot through her as the scar on her cheek split open. Talbot turned his attention to Yaro who had rolled over to see where the blow had come from. He saw Talbot lifting his sword high ready to strike down on him again. Yaro kicked out, ramming his boot into his assailant's groin. Talbot yelled and collapsed to the ground as Yaro aimed another heavy kick at his chest, sending him flying.

Silas and Caleb were matching each other blow for blow. They were oblivious to the fighting happening on the other side of the mast, each of them focussed solely on their opponent. The boat lurched sickeningly in the rough waves but the two combatants barely noticed. They'd each spent long enough at sea to have no trouble keeping their balance in the tricky conditions.

The contest on this side of the ship was very different to the unruly scrap happening between the others. Silas was an expert with the sword, his skills honed by years of piracy. But Caleb was no novice. His father had begun his training and then Captain Marmaduke had pushed him harder and further. They flung themselves around the deck as their weapons clashed again and again.

Then Caleb made a mistake, leaving his arm a fraction wide. Silas saw his chance and flicked his sword, knocking Caleb's arm further out as he followed it up with a punch with his free hand. The fist landed squarely on Caleb's jaw and sent him stumbling to the side of the ship. Only the rigging stopped him falling overboard, the triangular net of rope cushioning him.

Silas leapt after him but Caleb reacted quickly. Reaching for the ladder of rope above him he pulled himself up and kicked out with both feet. Silas dodged his boots but was thrown off balance. Caleb spun his body round as he dropped to the deck, his sword whipping towards Silas's neck. The pirate just got his own weapon up in time to make the block, the heavy jolt as the blades met sending shockwaves all the way up Caleb's arm.

Eloise spat blood to the floor and felt dazed as she tried to get to her knees. For a moment she thought the blow had caused stars to appear in her vision but as her eyes came back into focus she realised it was the blue and green jewels sliding around the deck, flickering in the light of the flames now spreading up the foremast. Some of the gems were spilling over the side, lost in the thundering water but there was nothing she could do about that now. She staggered to her feet using her sword as a crutch to push herself up. The ship rolled and sent her wobbling unsteadily to the edge of the boat where she had to grasp the rail to keep her balance as she watched the fire spread to the rigging on the side of the ship.

Lifting her sword she swung it through the flaming ropes, cutting them easily and temporarily halting the spread. Before she could put the fire out completely Ramsay's sword unexpectedly came out of nowhere and she had to duck as it swiped through the air above her head. He'd managed to pull himself out of the churning sea and clamber up the side. Eloise threw a punch at his head and felt a crunch as it connected with his nose. He almost lost his grip but held on and brought his sword up ready to strike.

Suddenly an arm appeared at his chest and she saw Jasper's face materialize . The young pirate wrapped himself around Ramsay and kicked away from the side of the ship sending both of them tumbling back into the sea.

Talbot had also recovered and was moving to attack Yaro again. Barrowclough was behind him, kneeling on Finlay's chest as he landed three big fists in succession. Yaro was still tied to him and was unable to stand to face Talbot without pulling Barrowclough away. Eloise, blood pouring from her left cheek, swayed from side to side as she tried to get to them. She reached the scrum and raised her own curved blade towards Talbot but then twisted at the last second and swung it down at Yaro.

Talbot was briefly stunned, looking at the sword falling in surprise, but then it shot straight past Yaro and sliced through the rope tying him to Barrowclough before ending its journey wedged in Finlay's side. Now free, Yaro stood to his full height. Eloise ripped her sword free of Finlay's body sending a plume of blood spraying across the deck as the doomed pirate curled up in agony. Barrowclough retrieved his discarded axe and the three of them all turned to face Talbot.

'Drop it, ya bilge-sucking son of a biscuit-eater,' growled Barrowclough menacingly.

Yaro picked up the sword dropped by Douglas and stepped towards Talbot. The pirate, outnumbered three to one, knew when to quit and threw his weapon at their feet. Yaro pushed him roughly to the ground and placed a boot on his back. 'You move, you die,' he threatened, holding the tip of his sword to Talbot's ear.

31

'It's over,' shouted Eloise, pointing her sword at Silas. The pirate spun round to see the devastation on the rest of the ship. Douglas was down, possibly dead. Finlay was on his knees, his hands clasped to his stomach, his trousers stained with blood. Talbot was flat to the floor with Barrowclough casually lifting and dropping the axe into the palm of his hand beside him. There was no sign of Ramsay. Eloise herself looked like the devil, one side of her face a mess of blood reflecting in the moonlight although he could see her sword was held firmly. Yaro, the muscular ex-slave hurried to douse the flames at the front of the ship. The foremast was black and cracked, with the remnants of the rigging smouldering beside it as wisps of smoke drifted up, but the flames themselves were now out.

Silas edged away from them all, finding himself trapped against the rigging at side of the ship. 'You think you've won?' he taunted, clutching onto the rigging with one hand as he aimed his sword at each of them in turn. 'I'll beat the lot of you. I'll feed your scurvy-ridden corpses to the fishes.' He suddenly swung himself up onto the rail so that he was towering above them all, one hand still on the ropes leading to the top of the mast, his other pointing his sword at the sky. 'I'll string you up by your necks and cut out your livers while you watch.'

A boom split the air making everyone on the deck jump. The Cutlass had seen Silas's signal and had now opened fire. The long unicorn horn bowsprit exploded at the front of the ship as the cannonball crashed through it. In the confusion Silas began quickly climbing the rigging. Too late, Caleb and Eloise both realised he was heading for Celeste who had been safely hiding from the fighting below.

'Get us away from the Cutlass,' shouted Caleb as he launched himself at the ropes. Eloise leapt for the rigging on the opposite side of the ship and began racing up.

'Weigh the anchor!' shouted Barrowclough, dropping his axe as he hurried to raise the mainsail. Yaro abandoned Talbot and ran to the back of the ship where it took all his effort to hoist the heavy iron anchor off the seabed.

Caleb went up the rigging like lightening. He'd trained for two years and was the fastest of the crew at scaling the ropes but Silas saw him coming and stamped on his hand. Caleb shouted out in pain as he let go, hanging dangerously by his other hand. As he hung there he saw Jasper being thrown around in the water below.

'Jasper!' he called. 'Get in the tender!' The sea

erupted as another cannonball landed nearby and Jasper swam madly towards the small boat tied to the ship. The Cutlass had changed course and was now coming straight towards them. Barrowclough had the sail half up and The Unicorn was slowly starting to move but they were sitting ducks. The larger pirate ship would be on top of them long before they'd be able to get any speed.

Celeste had seen Silas coming for her and raced up the mast to get away. The triangle of rope netting got narrower the higher she climbed. There was no crow's nest on this ship and when she got to the top there was nowhere to hide. A crossbeam stretched out on both sides with the great mainsail hanging below it. From here it looked like a very long way down. Nervously, Celeste stood on the crossbeam and stepped out, both hands still clinging on tightly to the mast.

She yelped as Silas climbed level with her and grabbed onto her wrist. Her foot slipped and she screamed as she fell, but Silas had her in his grip and she hung there helplessly.

'Not a step closer or I drop her,' he shouted to Caleb and Eloise.

Far below Yaro locked the anchor into position then ran to the wheel. 'Head towards shore,' called Barrowclough as another explosion went off behind them. The cannonballs were getting closer.

'Towards shore?' asked Yaro. 'It's a boat graveyard with these rocks.'

'Just do it,' Barrowclough shouted.

Yaro shook his head but did as the quartermaster ordered and turned them away from The Cutlass towards the island. A wave crashed into the stern. With the anchor raised there was nothing to keep them in place and they were carried suddenly forwards. A huge plume of spray shot into the air where they'd previously been as another cannon shot just missed them.

They felt a shudder rumble through the ship as they ran across a large rock hidden below the surface. Caleb anxiously watched Silas in case the shaking of the ship caused him to slip or to drop Celeste but the pirate held his footing until the obstacle passed and they eased back into clear water. The Cutlass had already halved the distance between them and was gaining fast as Yaro spun the wheel hard to port to throw their gunners off their aim. He was just in time. Another cannon boomed and the water on their starboard side burst as the heavy metal ball impacted.

'Call them off!' Caleb shouted to Silas. He was high up on the rigging, Eloise directly in front of him having climbed the other side. 'Or they'll kill you too.'

'I'm safe enough up here,' Silas laughed. 'They'll hit the ship soon but that will only stop us escaping. They'll board us long before she sinks.' Silas stepped onto the solid crossbeam, one hand on the mast and the other still dangling Celeste high above the deck. Caleb was directly below them on the port-side rigging. He coiled his foot around the rope square to make sure he was securely attached. If a cannonball hit them he didn't want to be thrown off.

Eloise quietly climbed the last few rungs of the rigging until she was level with Silas on the other side of the mast. 'Hand her to me,' she told him, holding out her hand. 'I'll tell you where the jewels are.'

Silas shook his head. 'You can't be trusted. The Duke should've taken you all them years ago instead of your brother, you'd have made a good pirate. But don't worry, I'll find the gems without your help. Any minute now, The Cutlass will scuttle this doomed tub and then you'll be begging me to let you live.'

A terrible crunching sound suddenly made them all turn. The Cutlass had risen into the air and was frozen suspended. It hung there for a few seconds then leaned precariously to one side, the black and scarlet skull and crossbones fluttering helplessly in the breeze.

'Look,' called Eloise. A gaping hole had appeared in the hull. Caught on the rocks, The Cutlass was being battered by the waves, its weakened keel twisted mercilessly by the relentless sea. With an earth-shattering crack she split open, water rushing into both the stern and the bow. The water frothed and bubbled as air escaped.

'No!' howled Silas. Stunned by the sight of his ship floundering he let go of Celeste's wrist.

The twins reacted at the same time. Caleb let go of the rigging with both hands and dove out to catch Celeste. Her arm was waving wildly as she plummeted but he reached out and clung onto it as she passed. His foot was still wrapped tightly to the rigging and their fall was halted abruptly. Caleb was left hanging upside down, Celeste swaying below him in his grasp.

In the same second Eloise swung herself around the mast and thrust her sword into Silas's chest. He gasped, his eyes wide with surprise as he looked at the ornate hilt wavering on the end of the curved steel, but then his lips curled into a snarl and he pulled out his own sword. Eloise reached forwards and dragged her blade back, blood spurting from the wound as she sliced down on Silas's wrist before he could strike. He snatched his hand away, letting go of the mast as he did so. The ship slammed into another wave and he wobbled uncertainly then almost in slow motion began to fall backwards. His hands scrabbled desperately for the mast but his fingers barely brushed it and then he was falling.

Caleb saw him coming and swung Celeste away in case he made a grab for her on the way down but he needn't have worried. Silas shot past them, arms and legs swinging as he fell. It seemed to take an age for him to finally smash into the water.

'Hold on,' Caleb called to Celeste. He was still hanging upside down by his ankle and heaved her towards the rigging. Eloise hurried down to join her as Caleb pulled himself upright.

'She's sinking fast,' he noticed, nodding towards The Cutlass. He was distracted by a hand appearing on the side of the ship below then let out a small cheer as Jasper appeared. When he looked back The Cutlass was gone. It had gone down so quickly the crew hadn't even had a chance to escape. They were still below decks manning the cannons and had gone to the bottom of the sea along with their ship. A few bits of wood and several barrels were all that was left.

Barrowclough steered them carefully away from the rocks and towards the deeper water as Caleb, Eloise and Celeste climbed down. They stood there silently watching the debris floating in the water where the pirate ship had last been.

The water suddenly ballooned as if a large bubble had risen to the surface. Everyone on board jumped as a huge wooden box burst into the air then settled in the water. It rolled gently up and down on the waves then a hatch opened in the top and the bearded head of Tarian, the ship's carpenter, popped up out of the crate. He saw Caleb on The Unicorn and gave a wave, then disappeared back inside. A moment later a mast rose out of the hatch and a small patchwork sail unfurled. Caleb followed Tarian's slow progress with amusement until the ship's carpenter finally pulled up alongside them.

'Permission to come aboard, captain,' called Tarian.

Caleb grinned. 'You'll have to ask her,' he replied, nodding at his sister.

'Ouch,' Tarian said, noticing the deep bloody gouge on Eloise's cheek. 'Looks like you'll need stitches in that. Got room for a ship's surgeon on your crew?'

'Throw him a rope,' smiled Eloise, gazing in wonder at the wooden contraption.

'Always knew there was a chance we'd run into trouble one day,' Tarian explained when he was safely on board. 'Built myself an escape pod in the bottom of the ship.' He looked down at it admiringly. 'Bit of a squeeze mind. And reckon I'll need to come up with something that sails a bit quicker next time.'

Caleb and Eloise looked at each other and laughed. A squeeze was putting it mildly. Caleb couldn't imagine how the enormous Tarian had fitted through the hatch in the first place.

'We might be in the market for a bigger ship if you want to build it into that?' suggested Eloise.

Tarian looked at them appraisingly then let out a long whistle when he saw the remaining emeralds still spread out around the deck. 'Ah, well, since you appear to have the funds, let me show you my idea for a new ship design. You'll like it, it's a twin.'

'A what?' asked Caleb.

'It's been at the back of my mind for a while,' Tarian replied. 'One ship, big and strong, but it can split in two if needed and sail independently. You two can take half each.'

Eloise looked at Caleb. 'What do you think, Captain Storm? Shall we sail the seas together?'

Caleb grinned. 'Aye aye, Captain Storm.'

Epilogue

As the new crew of The Unicorn gathered the scattered emeralds and set sail, the remnants of The Cutlass washed towards the shore. Night had fallen and in the darkness waves broke on the sandy beach and a colony of bats left their cave to hunt.

The high tide came and went, refilling the reservoir which hid the secret chamber holding the bulk of the treasure of the Emerald Sea. Any footprints left by Caleb and Eloise as they explored the tunnel had been washed away, erasing all evidence that they'd been there.

Further inland the long branch still sat on the surface of the quicksand. It had sunk slightly and now lay half submerged next to a long coat and a strange, three-cornered captain's hat. Unless they were disturbed they would remain where they were, tempting any curious explorers who wouldn't realise the danger lying beneath until it was too late.

A blue-headed hummingbird flew down and landed on the branch, its head twitching around as it tried to decide whether this was a safe place to spend the night. It could sense no predators and everything was still. The little bird's heart rate and breathing slowed as it settled into a deep sleep, but then a movement in the sand nearby startled it. Its head jerked left and right looking for threats but all had gone quiet again.

It jumped suddenly as a hand appeared out of the sand, launching itself into the air in search of a safer place to nest. The hand reached out and felt the branch, holding on as an arm gradually emerged. Slowly, ever so slowly, more followed, until finally the sand parted and a face burst into the cool night. The Duke breathed deeply, taking long, grateful gulps of air. It may take him a while, all night if necessary, but he knew now that he would make it out alive...

Printed in Great Britain
by Amazon